NEW BEGINNINGS

By

Sharon Downes

Acknowledgments

Huge thanks to my family and friends for their continued confidence that I would not only finish writing the book, but also that it would be funny.

To mum and dad thank you for the 'on tap' beverages when I was writing on my day off from my other job.

Thank you to my daughter, Laura for her insights into social media and marketing, and thank you to my son George for arranging for the fabulous illustrator, Moira Zahra to design the cover and for help delivering punchlines. I love you both to the moon and back.

I started writing the book early 2017 when my brother Jason had been diagnosed with Motor Neurone Disease. Writing this was my escape from facing the reality of the illness. Even when Jay was at his worst he still pushed me on, his belief in me never wavering. Sadly, in November 2017 he lost his battle with the disease. This book is dedicated to him.

And lastly, my wonderful husband Rob, for his never-ending support, comfort and constant cups of tea (and biscuits). Thank you just doesn't seem enough. The life changed for the better the day I met you (again).

Dedicated to

my wonderful brother Jason.

You were simply fabulous.

Your memory lives on in all of us.

PART ONE

THE END

Chapter 1

Everyone deals with grief differently. Whether it's the loss of a job, a loved one, a friendship or a marriage. Some people turn to their friends, family, or a professional and for some it might be the bottle. They might lock themselves away, not eating or sleeping. Their only comfort are the tears they shed and the memories they cherish. They stay in darkness, no energy to open the curtains and only just managing to feed the cat (obviously, provided they have a cat.), but don't get me wrong, it's not *all* negative - just think of the weight loss!

Me? Like most people I seek solitude, darkness and my duvet. Unfortunately, unlike most of the population who can't face food, all appetites vanished (what's that about?) I turn to food. Preferably of the chocolate variety but I'm not fussy.

The little voice in my head argues that it's *only* the chocolate kind, and that my idea of a balanced diet is a cup of tea in one hand and a packet of chocolate digestives in the other! Harsh but true. Yes, I admit I do turn to chocolate at times of crisis, joy, boredom, or when the sun/moon are up.

What can I say? I love chocolate, I crave chocolate, and on occasion, I sleep (and have been known to dream) chocolate. Food is my comfort blanket and when something bad happens, I shut down. I think I have Negative Narcolepsy. 'Lost my job? zzz. Argument with hubby? zzz. Put 10lb on over Christmas? zzz (Don't judge, it can happen.)

Anyway, you get the point. Like the song 'Eat, Sleep, Rave, Repeat', my version is more like, 'Eat (chocolate), Sleep, Crave (chocolate), Repeat'. Well, in my defence they don't specify what to eat, and it's working for me so sod it.

Anyway, back to the grief part. Andy, my darling husband of 28 years has departed. He has gone away. He is here no more …

Oh, he's not dead, in case you were wondering. The scumbag has run off with his young Australian physiotherapist, Zooey! The woman can't even spell her bloody name right. It's Z.O.E. for God's sake! Anyway, I guess he decided that I wasn't good enough, or clearly young enough. She's only 29. It's disgusting, she's the same age as our eldest daughter.

Andy said he wanted to feel young again and the daily grind/routine of work, kids and me (mainly me) was getting on top of him. I'm guessing that's what it was as our 'kids' are 29, 27 and 25 and a little far away to get on top of him. Molly (eldest) has moved to Bristol and is a working mum and married to Charles - born with a silver spoon in his mouth but we try not hold that against him. They have 2 gorgeous children, twins Sebastian and Amelia. They are adorable, but little monkeys when they set their mind to something and they're only 3. God help us when they get older. But, do you think that my deserter of a husband has given a second thought to those poor little souls? You can bet your Spanx he's not.

As for work, Andy owns a very successful property development company which we set up over 25 years ago, so now he's got staff he isn't as busy as he used to be. Well, who can find the time when you're a cheating scumbag rat? Sorry, I've digressed.

Ellie, our middle child lives with her partner, Jackie and works as a Supervisor at a mini Tesco in a little town in Manchester. That's where Jackie's from. She's a security officer for the same Tesco and I've got to admit it was a bit of a shock when Ellie 'came out', but once you see how happy she is, does it really matter that they're the same sex? Everyone has differing opinions, but for me if Ellie's happy then I'm happy.

Billy, the baby of the family – OK I know he's 25 - lives in Edinburgh where he's at University doing his Master's in Zoology or something. I get the impression that he would like to be a student forever. Crushed, I asked him once could he not have moved any further away from me? (Billy's answer was, 'Shetland don't have a university.') Cheeky sod.

So, back to me. I'm sat here in Andy's old dressing gown which smells so much of him I can't take it off. I'm being pathetic I know, but I feel lost and this soothes me. It's like knowing he's here but I don't have to make his tea. (Embarrassingly, I'd love to make his tea again.)

Anyway, I'm slowly working my way through another packet of chocolate digestives and a brew and when I've done that I'm going back to bed, pulling the duvet over my head and imagining I'm lay in the sunshine, tanning my pasty white body and listening to the waves wash up on the shore.

He's been gone 3 weeks now. The kids keep saying he'll be back, but I don't think so, and after this long would I want him back? The stronger voice in my head shouts, 'not bloody likely' but the whiney voice, the real me, coming from my heart whimpers, 'of course I would' and I start crying all over again.

So, in a nutshell I'm not getting any better and I'm starting to look like Rocky at the end of his films (I'd have just given up boxing if I was him). I'm just getting fatter, puffier and whiter by the day, I'm sure I have scurvy and the Tesco delivery driver thinks I have shares in McVities.

I've not stepped out of the house once, obviously because I'm still wearing his threadbare dressing gown and I haven't showered since he told me his news, but the shame of bumping into anyone (in said dressing gown and smelling like the bin lorry) would be too much to bear.

The kids have been great. It's hard with them all living so far away, and they have their own lives and jobs and can't just run to me when I need them, but it would have been nice. I know Molly is busy with work and the twins and she does ring me most days, which I appreciate. It's the same with Ellie – minus the kids and Billy is busy studying but, in fairness he only rings when he wants me to loan him some money. When I say loan, I mean give. There's no use pretending anymore. But, for the first time ever, I've said no and he'll have to ask his dad. 'Go you!' I hear you chant, but no it's not because I'm being strong, it's purely because my money is needed for my shares in McVities.

So, I just sit here on the sofa with no energy to do anything. Not shower, not get dressed, not do anything. Back to 'Eat, sleep, crave, repeat.

I'm floating down a large staircase wearing the most stunning ivory dress. Andy is at the bottom of the stairs looking gorgeous in a black tuxedo with a look of adoration on his face, like he used to when we first got married. I look like Jessica Rabbit, but the dress is in ivory. I am sexy, I am strong, I am all woman. I take a step down but miss the top step and suddenly I'm tumbling down, down, down the stairs and my dress has turned into a huge sheet of ivory satin that I'm wrapped up in and can't get out and I'm still falling …

That's when I wake up on the floor. I've managed to get the blanket from the sofa tangled in my legs and the dressing gown, and then fallen off the sofa.

The image of Andy was so clear in my dream that I could even smell him - although that could be the dressing gown - and it's made me all teary again. Worst still, I've run out of soft tissues and am now forced to blow my nose on scratchy kitchen roll. On the plus side, one sheet does do plenty.

I think back to when Andy and I met. We were in secondary school and I had the biggest crush on him, with his long fringe of black hair and dark eyes. He was the coolest guy in our year and even though he wasn't that tall he was drop dead gorgeous. Sadly, he didn't even notice me until we got to 4th year (and my boobs came in or rather popped out) and then, funnily enough, he did. Maybe it was a sign of things to come.

He asked me to be his girlfriend then, well he sort of asked me; he asked his mate to ask my mate if I would go out with him. Tut boys, honestly, they are so immature.

So, naturally being the far more superior sex, I told my mate to tell his mate … yes. What a complicated life we led as teenagers.

He was so lovely and couldn't have been happier. There I was, average Amanda, girlfriend to one of the coolest boys in school. He would send me romantic little notes in class like:

'Meet me after school behind the bike shed'

'I'll knock on for you tonight.'

'Your tits look MASSIVE today!!'

Well erm scrap the last one, anyway you get the gist. We fell madly in love with each other – he grew to 5ft 9" and I managed 5ft 4" at a stretch – and since then have, or rather had been together for 33 years until…. well, until we weren't. Doing the maths that makes me 47 and separated. Possibly even about to become divorced. Then I'll be a single, 47-year-old cat woman (must buy cat) who is addicted to chocolate and won't step out of the front door!

I wonder, do solicitors do house calls?

Chapter 2

I hear the key in the door and leap up spilling tea and biscuit crumbs everywhere. Oh my God, Andy can't see me like this. I look like Ken Dodd! But no, it's not him, it's just my best friend Chrissie. I return to my slouchy position on the couch and I silently curse the day I gave her a key, but she has been so patient with me (especially as I've been ignoring her), so I swallow my frustration. Chrissie is from Manchester and is not a wallow-er and I needed to wallow.

'Mandy are you in here luv?' She bellows, even though it's not that big a house and I'm not bloody deaf. 'For fuck's sake woman, it smells like a pigsty in here!' She does tend to exaggerate, I huff as she starts opening curtains and windows.

'God Chrissie, you've burned my retinas!' I hiss like a vampire being shown daylight. I groan and cover my eyes with one arm. Nosferatu has nothing on me.

She sees me then for the first time, sat (or rather slouched) on the couch, in Andy's old dressing gown surrounded by crumbs and biscuit wrappers and half-drunk cups of tea (who drinks all the way to the bottom? You don't know what's lurking there) and her face shows her shock. I can see she's visibly shaken by my appearance as when she comes to sit beside me, she changes her mind at the last minute, I guess the crumbs put her off.

'Oh, sweetheart you poor thing.' She pulls me up and tries to give me a hug, but steps back quickly. I guess she's nasally shaken as well.

'Eugh, for fuck sake, you smell bloody awful. And what the hell is that in your hair?' she reaches over and pulls half a chocolate digestive out from the greasy tangles.

'Right! This has gone too far. Mandy, he's not dead, although it's a definite possibility if I see the bastard. Look, he's left you, and don't say anything,' Like I'd get a chance. Manchester women don't mince their words and Chrissie comes across as a builder when she's angry. 'I know it feels like your life is over and you'll never be happy again, but you will! It's not like you've suddenly found out you've got some terminal illness or anything … Oh shit, I mean you haven't have you?' For a second, she looks worried, but when she sees my expression she continues.

'Right, that's it. Get your arse up those stairs and into that shower or so help me I'm bringing the hose pipe in and I'll fuckin' do it right where you're sat!'

As you can gather, she's not the most tactful woman in the world. You wouldn't believe she's a bereavement counsellor, would you? That's how we met. We work together and she's genuinely amazing at her job (and she doesn't swear). She's just crap with everyone else. Tact and diplomacy are not her top skills.

I stand up, but that just brings on a wave of panic and I sit back down as emotion takes over and the tears come.

'What am I going to do?' I cry, 'I can't bear it Chrissie, he's doing all sorts with a woman with a younger body, who hasn't had children and I still miss him so much. I can't live without him.'

I've been crying for so long and my eyes are so swollen I can hardly see, and now I have snot running down towards my mouth, and oh my god, was that a snot bubble that just came out of my nose? By Chrissie's expression I think it was. She hands me a piece of kitchen roll and tells me to blow my nose. 'Seriously Chrissie,' I sniff. 'He was my everything and now everyone will know he's left me for a young bloody Australian Physiotherapist called Zooey.'

'How?'

'What?'

'How will they know?' she asks logically. 'Do you plan on walking up and down High Street wearing a fuckin' sandwich board emblazoned with the words 'THE BASTARD HAS LEFT ME FOR A YOUNG

AUSTRALIAN PHYSIOTHERAPIST!'? No, you're fuckin' not!' I hate it when she has logic on her side.

'But look at my swollen eyes!'

'Wear sunglasses and tell people it's conjunctivitis.'

'And my big red nose?' I blow my nose again to emphasise my point.

'For fuck sake, you've had a bad cold. Now is there anything else?' She is now stood with her hands on her hips, eyes just begging me to argue with her. This woman can be quite scary at times.

'OK, fine. You win. I'll have a shower. And there's no need to swear so much!' I shout and stomp upstairs like a stroppy teenager.

'AND KEEP YOUR HANDS OFF MY BISCUITS!'

After I've showered, shaved my armpits and legs (I was beginning to look like a Wookie) and washed and dried my hair, admittedly I feel a bit better. I've even put a little make up on, not that it's going to work miracles, but making me look better than Rocky, shows that the impossible is … possible.

I go downstairs, and I see that Chrissie has worked miracles herself. She's hoovered all my crumbs up and thrown away all the empty wrappers and wiped all the tea rings from most available surfaces. All the dishes have been loaded in the dishwasher and it's humming nicely. The air smells better, she must have found the air freshener. I think I must have gone 'nose blind'. But, my home looks normal again and it's all thanks to my amazing friend.

'Right, we're going out for lunch.' Chrissie announces before I'm able to thank her for being great.

'Oh Chrissie, no I can't. I've not been out for weeks and look at me!' I've started to panic breathe. A lot of breaths in and not many out.

'Somewhere swish…. How about Harper's?' she continues as though I haven't spoken.

'No, no, no. I'm staying here and besides it gets busy in there and I'm not that hungry and what if I bump into someone I know? Can't we just go to the M&S cafe?'

'What a load of bollocks!' she says in her usual diplomatic way. 'So what if you bump into someone you know? Either smile and say you'd love to chat but you've got to get on, or just tell them to piss off and mind their own business.' She smiles at me knowing full well that I don't swear and would never be so rude. 'Now, get your shoes on, we're going out and did you really just suggest M&S?' She shakes her head in despair.

I will admit that although I was sulking like a petulant teenager, reminiscent of Kevin and/or Perry, it was nice to be out. Lunch was delicious, I was obviously hungrier than I thought. The seafood linguine was amazing, and Chrissie tucked into her spaghetti carbonara with gusto, so I'm guessing she enjoyed it, and to top it off I haven't seen anyone I know.

Conversation has always been natural and easy with the pair of us and I thank her from the bottom of my heart for getting me off my … erm … bottom, and for making me feel human again and to be honest, things seem a little easier. In fact, I'm positively glowing - although I do think that's the wine.

'You know I really appreciate you taking my clients on for the last few weeks. Were they OK? I will be back soon, I promise.' I still want to hide under my duvet, but she's been amazing and it's only fair on Chrissie and my clients that I get back to work.

'Don't worry about it love, that's what mates are for and you know I'll do anything for you.' She says magnanimously. 'But you owe me big time and you'll be back Monday, no fuckin' buts!' She firmly informs me. Maybe not quite the altruistic gesture I initially thought then.

After lunch Chrissie insists on some retail therapy and enlightens me on the positive side of becoming newly single. I love her optimism.

'There are several joys from getting divorced. (She has been divorced 3 times, so I bow to her expert knowledge.)

1. No more duvet stealing
2. Full control of the TV remote
3. Less washing/ironing
4. Current access to your joint bank account
5. You can do what you want. Especially with current access to joint bank account!

Andy owns a very successful property development company which makes executive homes. After we finished school, he did a building course at college and started from there. We came into some money when my dad passed away. I wanted to buy a house, but Andy persuaded me there was enough to buy some land and build a couple of houses. I'm so glad he won that argument as things just escalated from there.

Chrissie is adamant that we go shopping while we can and spend some of our money. 'Stops the prick spending it on his fuckin' Aussie Physio Bitch 'Zooey' anyway'. She says with a wicked grin made even more wicked as she sees me blushing again at her language but, she does raise a valid point.

The thing is though, I hate shopping (for clothes, not food. I can shop for England when it comes to food). Don't get me wrong, when I say hate, I mean utterly, absolutely detest. I'm a size 18 and clothes shopping brings me out in hives. I tend to go for online shopping, where I can just send it back if I don't like it or it doesn't fit, and I like baggy and comfy. Unfortunately, Chrissie pleads a very strong case (basically bullies me) and so after another glass of wine or two, I agree.

My mind does begin to wander though, thinking about a possible divorce and the changes that are coming. To be honest, I've always dreamt of a little cottage by the sea with a lovely garden and I might even get a dog and call it Milly. On second thoughts I don't think the kids will be thrilled… Molly, Ellie, Billy and Milly? Maybe I'll work on the name. Oh, what about work though? I'd need to find a job and there aren't that many around, especially in my field. No, stop that now, be positive - people die all the time so counsellors are needed! Comforted by that 'morbid', yet practical thought I feel slightly more uplifted. There *is* a future to be had away from here.

Back to reality, shopping first. Unfortunately, as a curvy size 18 it's not always easy to shop for clothes.

Reasons for hating shopping

- Nothing sleeveless – fat arms continue to wobble long after I've stopped waving
- Nothing too short – fat knees
- Nothing too tight – bum stands out
- Nothing too bright – don't want the rest of me to stand out

Unfortunately, Chrissie is having none of my negativity so it's Harvey Nicks, Selfridges and John Lewis. Argh!

After all that stressing (albeit only for about 30 minutes) today seems to be my lucky day. As I've lived off nothing but tea and biscuits for three weeks it turns out I've lost a little weight (I don't recommend that diet though, my skin is a mess and I've probably got scurvy) but the clothes fit so much better and some of the stretchy items are even size 16! If they did a size 17 it would be perfect.

By the time I'm done I've bought so many things, I need to consider re-mortgaging the house or selling a kidney. Andy will go berserk when he checks the account. My arms are laden with shopping bags and my bounty consists of:

- 2 handbags – these always fit
- 3 pairs of shoes – no explanation needed
- 2 dresses – figure hugging and do not come under the comfortable category
- 3 blouses – same as above.
- A gorgeous pair of ivory trousers that are so flattering that even I had a second look at my bum

in them, so naturally I bought them in black and navy too. Well, you can't miss an opportunity like that, can you?

- And, … drum roll … the first pair of jeans I've had in over 20 years.

It doesn't stop there though. I, Amanda Harper, have booked a holiday! It's only a week in the UK and not backpacking across the Himalayas, but it's in a gorgeous cottage in Port Isaac in Cornwall. (Might as well check out my retirement home.) Chrissie said I needed to get away from it all, and we're not short of a penny or two so I booked it. To be honest, I feel amazing! This morning I could have been mistaken for a homeless person and now I'm like a new woman, strutting through the town like Julia Roberts in Pretty Woman, laden not just with eyebags, but shopping bags full of clothes, shoes etc. Nothing is going to stop this feeling. Nothing at all!

Until I get home and the enormity of what I've done AND spent has hit me and sent me into a panic of which I've never experienced before. The tears come in one huge torrent. There's only one thing for it.

Where are those biscuits?

Chapter 3

I t's been a couple of weeks since the shopping trip and the weather has been getting nicer as we're well into spring. Although living up north it does mean that it might still snow.

I swap between feeling like I'm drowning and can't come up for air; all I can see in my head is her young flexible body, to feeling strong and determined. I'm still in shock and can't believe that a couple of months ago everything was OK. At least I thought we were OK.

He *was* working late a lot, but he said he had to since the recession hit, so it just became the norm. It just meant that I had a fair few evenings to myself and after 33 years it came as a blessing some nights. But that said, I would never, ever in a million years think that he would leave me. I'm not being naïve or anything but, we were just a normal couple and he was 'My Andy'.

We'd been together so long that we just seemed to mould into one. We laughed together, or we used to. We made love. Well actually I can't remember the last time we did that either (that's normal though after being with someone for so long, isn't it?). He just says he's too tired after work and recently he's needed regular physio for his bad shoulder. God! What a fool I've been. So bloody naïve. OK be tough, be strong, be confident ... be ... be more like Chrissie.

I've been back at work for a few weeks and that's helped. It's a lot easier to forget your own problems when you're hearing someone else's. My clients range from a poor young woman whose baby was stillborn, to a lady who recently lost her Bracco Italiano (Apparently, it's a dog and not her Mediterranean lover – I won't make that mistake again).

On a positive note, my trip to Cornwall is just 2 weeks away and I'm getting a little excited. Andy never really liked holidays in England, he always preferred being abroad somewhere hot, provided they had an English pub nearby he could sit in. I never quite understood that. In my mind if you go to another country you try their food, experience their culture and learn a little of their history. I could sit for ages outside a cafe just people watching and when the children were younger I would take them around the cities and not just to the beaches. Old architecture has always fascinated me. The way buildings were made, hundreds of years ago and with none of the modern technology we have today. How creative and intelligent those architects of old were.

Sometimes I'd draw or paint, not that they were that good, but I loved art at school and I just carried on doing it. I used to do more but at some point, I just stopped.

Andy never appreciated that and would rather have a pint, eat burger and chips, watch the football and play darts and I never complained as it meant, on the plus side, that I got to do pretty much what I wanted. He had his sport and the shade. Andy was quite fair skinned so didn't really like beaches, in fact we used to joke that it would take him a week of sunbathing just to go white.

Today, work wasn't too bad, and traffic was light, so I get home at a reasonable time. The postman has left me a couple of flyers; one for new windows (apparently you buy one, you get one free!) and one about a local slimming class (ha), and there's a letter from a solicitor. My hands shake as I open the letter and my heart breaks all over again. Andy is officially filing for divorce on the grounds of irreconcilable differences. I didn't even know there were any differences to reconcile in the first place. Tears blur my eyes as I try to read what's in the letter. More shocking, he wants to sell the house and is offering me 50% of the profit, 50% of his pensions and he will continue to pay the bills until the house is sold.

I know he'd left but I didn't expect it to go this far, this quick and it's not 'the house' it was our home! And I know we'd agreed it was too big for us now but still, it's not the point. I still have marks on the doorframe in the kitchen of how much the kids grew each birthday. I was running out of door frame by the time Billy left home. Our lovely, beautiful little family grew here. Our home is full of so many memories and as I walk around I remember them all with sadness now. We shared some hard times but some amazing times too. How can he do this?

I am numb. This is real and there's no getting away from it. I can't pretend that I'm going to wake up one morning and it's all been a dream and Andy will be in the shower. No, this isn't Dallas, this is Cheshire, and I am one extremely sad housewife of Cheshire.

I am so worked up that I don't even go to the biscuits, I go to the phone and ring Chrissie. She knows everything. Unfortunately, I ring the Chinese chippy twice as my hands are shaking so much, but when she answers and hears mumble 'solicitor' and 'letter' in between my great racking sobs, she calms me down and promises to be round in the next half hour.

I need to keep busy as I'm sick of crying and there's only so much Crème de la Mer can do, so I put some washing on (NOT the dressing gown), hoover downstairs, dust the dust-free lounge and hallway and re-arrange the Cheshire Life magazines artistically on the table just how Andy liked them. Then I mess them up again, just because I can. I'm just putting the kettle on when Chrissie walks in.

'Come here,' she gives me a big cuddle and the floodgates open, again, and I sob like a baby in her arms. After a few minutes asking if I'm OK, which I sniff a snotty yes (thankfully minus the snot bubble this time), she tells me to put my 'fuckin' face straight (a northern colloquialism which in this instance is a gesture of love) and get the kettle on for a brew (another colloquialism) as we've got work to do.

From her enormous tote bag, she produces a calculator, a pen and a large yellow pad like the ones solicitors use. Maybe she bought some ready for her next divorce – I mean she's not met him yet, but she does like to be organised. I just get on with making the tea and eating the biscuits.

'OK, first things first, show me the letter.' I hand it over saying that I think he's being quite generous really. She looks at me as though I've just sprouted antennae and threatened to probe her, she turns away shaking her head, puts her glasses on and reads the letter, all the while tutting and making notes on her yellow pad. You'd think she really was a solicitor the way she's acting.

I've made the tea, that's all I seem able to do, except nervous eat biscuits (but that's a given). I sit down with Chrissie and put her cup in front of her with 4 spoons of sugar (urgh, I think it's the sugar that keeps her going). 'Don't worry I didn't stir it, I know you don't like it sweet ha ha … erm … ha'. It's a very weak attempt at humour but she's making me nervous with all the tutting and writing. 'Well?' I ask.

'Hmmm' she answers. 'It's not a bad offer but he's not mentioned the one thing that's obviously, fuckin' blatantly, missing.' I look back at her with a totally blank expression as I have no clue as to what she's talking about.

'His bastard business!' she shouts.

'His business?' I'm lost and look it. I close my mouth as it's not the most flattering look.

'Yes love,' she says, looking at me like I should know this. 'You're obviously entitled to part of that too. He's tried to make it look like he's being Mr Generosity himself when in fact he is shafting you in the arse!'

'*He's WHAT???*' I cough up my tea and choke a little.

'Sorry Mandy love, you know what I mean though. Look, who gave him the money to set it up?'

'Well, it was from….' But I'm not given a chance to answer.

'You.' She says and continues straight on. 'Who was there supporting him when he set up business on his own?'

'Err, it was….'

'You.' At this point she's on a roll and even though I now know the answers I realise I'm not actually meant to answer her questions, so I led her plod on.

'Who was there supporting him when he set up business on his own? You. Who gave him 3 amazing children and still did all his invoicing and tax returns? Fuckin' you. Who chased up debtors and pushed suppliers when they were letting him down? FU-CKING YOU! And all that while you were studying psychology and raising a family.'

She's got herself into a full-on lather and is red faced and a bit sweaty now, but she's not going to let that deter her from her soapbox glory. 'So, again who the fuck did ALL that?'

There's an uncomfortable pause and she's just looking at me with raised eyebrows.

'Me?' I say in what even I admit is a pretty pathetic voice, but I wasn't expecting to have to answer.

'YES, FUCKING YOU!' she shouts and bangs the table like Judge Judy. 'You really can be too nice at times.'

She passes me a card with the names Jones, Crimble and Harris Solicitors. Specialists in Marital Law.

'I've made you an appointment for tomorrow morning at 11.00 with Mr Harris. He's a gem and will sort you out no problem at all.' Looking chuffed to mint balls, and less red, she takes a big drink of her tea and spits it back in the cup – she's a classy lady my Chrissie. 'Fuck me Mand, you forget the sugar??'

Oops, maybe I did forget to stir it after all.

It's the following morning. I slept fitfully, dreaming that I was in court and I was so tiny compared to everyone else and everyone was eating chocolate biscuits and laughing that I wasn't getting anything, and I'd be sleeping on the streets like a homeless person. Then his giant Aussie bitch stood up to laugh and banged her hand down so hard on the table … then I woke up.

Oh my God, that felt so real. I'm wet through and my hair is stuck to my head. Breath slowly I tell myself as I lie here having palpitations, slowly in and out, in and out, in and out. After I've calmed myself down I put on my *own* dressing gown – Chrissie literally dragged Andy's off me and after a short tug of war (which obviously, she won) she took it outside and locked it in her car, not trusting that I wouldn't have taken it out of the bin and put it straight back on. God, what does she take me for? I would have aired it first.

After a cuppa and some toast, I shower and do my hair and makeup and look semi human again. I dress in my lovely new ivory trousers and a pastel coloured floaty top which is quite flattering. I complete the outfit with my new strappy nude sandals and handbag. I feel a little confident. No, I feel good, not great, but good is … erm good enough.

Chrissie has told me which paperwork I would need to take with me. Mortgage agreement, bank statements and some other things so, armed with that I go to meet my solicitor Mr Harris. I'm so nervous.

I'm not sure what I expected but the office is in a lovely old building in Chester's town centre. The receptionists are polite and very smart, if a little snooty and harsh looking (like when you need to go to the doctors and you have to go through the Gestapo just to get to see the GP). I felt uncomfortable telling them I was there to see Mr Harris as they would know that I'd failed as a wife and no wonder he'd left me, but I remind myself that they don't know the details of exactly *why* I'm here (and it's none of their business – shouts Chrissie's voice in my head). Either way I'm still nervous and I sit picking at my nails and trying not to make eye contact with them.

The phone rings. 'Mr Harris will see you now' says the most severe of the two. She stands up and, bloody hell she looks about 7-foot-tall, which is a slight exaggeration but only slight, she's huge and towers above me. 'If you would like to walk this way.' She says with aloofness. If only!

She sashays in front of me in her 4-inch heels. I've not been able to walk like that since 1989, and who wears 4-

inch heels in general, let alone for work? Bloody hell I'm so out of my depth I need armbands just to keep afloat.

'Lurch' knocks on the door and a voice shouts, 'come in'. For the first time in this whole experience I smile. Mr Harris is not what I was expecting at all. He's not 70 years old, slightly rotund with white hair and glasses perched on the end of his nose. I'm not sure where I got that image from, but he's about my age and is rather good looking. (Is it bad that I'm thinking that?)

He stands up to shake my hand, and I see that he's over 6ft tall with dark hair that is slightly greying at the temples and the brightest blue eyes I've ever seen. In fact, up close he's gorgeous. Abruptly he lets go of my hand and I don't know if he could feel it too but there was something odd when he touched my hand (a bit like supermarket shopping trolleys when you get that static shock, or maybe he's wearing some odd shoes that pick-up friction from the carpet). Anyway, I'm quite relieved when he lets go, that was nothing like I was expecting when I got here.

'Take a seat and don't mind Sarah,' he says about the Amazonian. 'She's always like that.' He laughs good-heartedly and his bright blue eyes twinkle like stars on pools and little laughter lines appear at the side of his eyes. Whoa, wait a god damn minute lady! You are here about a divorce, not to go all googly eyes over the first good looking guy you speak to. Twinkly eyes like pools indeed – my sensible head says. Phwoarr – the lower part of my body says (tingling). I give myself a mental shake and put it down to nerves, or thrush.

'OK, Chrissie has filled me on bits of your situation, but if you can tell me yourself what's happened we can then decide together how we are going to proceed.' He smiles warmly, and twinkles (STOP IT WOMAN!).

I'm so nervous, I start rambling. 'Thank you for agreeing to see me at such short notice Mr Harris, I do appreciate it. I ... erm ... I imagine you are very busy and I do appreciate this.' Crap, I've already said that. You are not a 16-year-old girl with a crush, even though that's exactly how this feels which is unnerving to say the least.

'Please call me Phil, my dad was Mr Harris.' He says, his voice gentle but strong. 'And, that's what I'm here for.'

So, I tell him everything that's happened. From Andy leaving me for Zooey, the young Australian Physiotherapist, (I leave the bitch part out – I don't want to look catty) all the way through to receiving the letter from his solicitor yesterday. I give him the letter with Chrissie's notes, which he laughs at saying that she was in the wrong profession and he buzzes Scary Spice for some tea for us both.

After a few minutes, she enters and places the tray on the desk and asks if I would like her to pour. Thankfully, Phil says he'll do it and I am so grateful for that tiny act alone. He asks how I take it. My brain kicks in before I blurt out 'any way you want to give it'. I must get out more.

'Just milk please.' I mumble.

'OK, let's look at your options. First, you can't divorce immediately unless your husband can prove unreasonable behaviour on your behalf so I'm not entirely sure what your husband's solicitor is talking about.'

'What?' I blurt out in shock. 'Unreasonable behaviour on MY part? I haven't done anything wrong. He just told me he was leaving me for an Australian bloody -sorry- young bloody -sorry- Australian physiotherapist called Zooey! Can you believe she spells it Z.O.O.E.Y? Who does that?' I know I have a bad case of verbal diarrhoea, but I can't help it. Thankfully, Phil takes it in his stride. I guess I'm not the first near hysterical woman he's had in his office. 'I mean he just told me one day that he was leaving, and he left, and I haven't heard from him since. I've been a loyal wife for 28 years. 28! And for what?' I'm sweating now I've gotten myself so worked up and tears fill my eyes, spilling onto my cheeks.

'It will be fine.' Soothes Phil, passing me a box of tissues. 'You've obviously had quite a shock and it will take some time to get used to it, but please don't worry, I'm here to help and together we can get you through this.' He hands me a cup of tea and calmly carries on, 'Please understand, your husband has no grounds whatsoever to divorce you. He would have to prove that you have done something that neither one of you can reconcile. You on the other hand can file for divorce based on adultery. Obviously, the bill then comes to you but if he's so desperate to get divorced then I'm sure he'll be happy to pay. Regarding your home though, your children are no longer dependants, but adults with their own lives so legally and unfortunately, your husband can request that the house is put on the market. As there is no mortgage the profit would be split 50/50. Obviously, you can buy him out, or he may want to buy you out and move into it himself.'

The tears start falling again. I can't help it, even though the house is too big for me and I was considering downsizing, it's still a shock to hear it said out loud. The possibility that he may consider moving in with *her* just gives me something else to worry about.

Phil does confirm that I'm entitled to half Andy's pension, but likewise he's entitled to half mine, although mine isn't so big as I was home with the kids for quite a few years. If we sell the house, we would each end up with quite a large sum of money. We bought the house when the children were little, so the mortgage is paid up, and if you add that to half the pension I know I would be able to start again. It sounds OK but it's just too much to process. I need to talk to my children about it all. As for the business, he says that will be harder to sort out, but I am entitled to some of the profit as we set it up together when we were younger. He asked if I was on any of the paperwork, any loans in my name etc. I can't honestly remember as my mind has gone blank with information overload, I now look like those nodding dogs you put in your car, but I tell him I'll check.

We end the appointment with the agreement that Mr Harr ... I mean Phil, will write to Andy's solicitor and introduce himself and let them know that they will be hearing from us shortly with our terms.

He holds out his hand for me to shake again and I notice it's surprisingly rough for a 'pen pusher'. (It's an odd thing to notice I know, especially when my whole world is falling apart, but I'm not thinking straight right now so you'll have to forgive me.) His look lingers as he says goodbye, but at this point I'm too upset to bother reading anything into it (although saying it here totally negates that comment). Anyway, we agree to meet in a few weeks when I've had time to search for the documents he mentioned. In the meantime, I'm going home, closing the curtains and getting my biscuits.

Chapter 4

It's been a couple of days since I met with my solicitor and I still can't believe that things have come this far so quickly. I'm devastated. Every time I hear someone near the door I think it's Andy coming back. I know some of you will be shaking your heads and telling me I'm better off without the cheating rat but to tell the truth, I miss him. We had been together for so long that I was just used to him, like comfy slippers or your favourite chair. Maybe that's not the best analogy, but I guess that could be where it started going wrong.

When we were first married he used to come home and wrap his arms around me and kiss me hello. Granted that was before 3 children, work and life took over. I'm not even sure when it changed to a peck on the cheek and a casual enquiry of what was for dinner. And that's only when he *did* come home. But, do you know what? It was still normal. Our routine. Good or bad, that's what I was used to.

When I think back I've always thought I was lucky. The perfect husband, the perfect family, the perfect house. I'm not saying that my children were angels and Andy and I never argued, but it was still *my* perfect family.

My friends used to be so jealous of us as we were always laughing with each other and they would moan at their husbands to be more like Andy. I guess they're more appreciative of what they've got now.

I'm not complacent or overly confident (I think you've probably worked that out by now) but I never, EVER would have imagined he would cheat. I'm not saying I'm too gorgeous or anything, it's just that it wasn't Andy. He was a family man, a provider, a loving dad, a loving husband, my friend, my lover, my world. How did it go so wrong?

Don't misunderstand me, it wasn't always sunshine and roses. Blimey, when we were first together we argued incessantly but we always made up vigorously.

Mum said that we had enough passion in our relationship that if we could bottle it we would make a fortune. When I had to tell her that Andy had left me, you'd have thought he'd left her. It took me ages to calm her down. But, once she was calm she was furious with him. I think she'd have given him a good wallop if she saw him. Mum used to say we could weather any storm that came and over the years I believed it. Sadly, we were both wrong.

Being so happy though in my own relationship meant it was so hard to watch Chrissie go through divorce after divorce. Please don't get me wrong I'm not saying she's a money grabbing gold digger. Ha, none of them had any money.

Her first husband Gordon was a decorator and a secret gambler, not so secret when bailiffs came to the door. He blamed it all on Chrissie and said she'd pushed him into it. So, divorce number one.

Next, Gary. He was an assistant manager at a local DIY branch. I'm not allowed to discuss which one but 'You Can Do It If You … It!' Basically, he cheated on her with Rhonda from the paint section and Julie from Tiling. So, divorce number 2.

Bastard, (sorry, I think Chrissie's rubbing off on me) I meant husband number 3 Lee came, and he was lovely. He was a hairdresser and simply fabulous. Unfortunately, a very confused gay hairdresser who hoped that getting married would straighten him out (pardon the pun), but sadly for Chrissie it didn't, and he cheated too with a guy called Roy who was a married builder with 3 children. I think his wife was slightly more shocked than Chrissie. (You couldn't make this stuff up.) So, divorce number 3.

The hardest part was watching Chrissie suffer. She's a mouthy bolshie Manchester lass on the outside and a loving softie on the inside.

Andy and I would lie in bed at night and say that would never be us and we'd cuddle up in each other's arms re-affirming just how strong we were. We knew each other inside out and had been through some tough times. When the recession hit we lived on beans on toast for so long that we joked it was 'the windy years'.

Andy and I had been together since we were 14, and after 4 years were desperate to live together but our parents forbade it saying we were too young. Which looking back we were, but naturally we knew best so we secretly booked our wedding at the local register office.

We were both 18 so needed no one's permission. We told each of our parents that we were staying at the other parent's house, therefore giving them no reason to be suspicious. And so, on a very blustery Wednesday on 21st September 1988 at 2.00 pm we got married with our two best friends as witnesses. We stayed in a travel lodge for our wedding night after having dinner in the Little Chef next door. It wasn't the most romantic wedding, but we certainly made the most of the wedding night. We were now officially Mr and Mrs Harper and grinning like we'd won the Pools, we made our way home to announce it to the world (by which I mean our parents.)

When we got home, our euphoria evaporated faster than a fairy liquid bubble. Our parents were furious and devastated. We had selfishly taken a special day away from them and we could never replace it. Where were we going to live? (We didn't think of that). What were we going to live off? (Didn't think of that either). Did we have jobs? (There's a definite pattern forming here). I had never felt so guilty or confused in my life.

When everything calmed down and we talked (or rather we listened) we moved in with my parents and got jobs part time around our college courses. I worked in a bar a few nights a week and Andy stacked shelves on the graveyard shift at the local Co-op. By the time we finished college, we had enough money for a deposit on a rented flat in the town and bought a few essentials. Our parents saw that we meant business and had worked hard for what we had, so at that point they both helped a little more. Mum and Dad gave us enough money for a sofa and a bed and Andy's parents paid for a washer and fridge freezer. We felt so posh in our little flat and life felt perfect.

Andy got himself a job as a labourer on a building site and I went into temping for some extra money to save for a deposit on a house. I put my dreams of University on hold as we needed the money for other things. 12 months later we had saved enough and with a little extra help from our parents we put a deposit down on a lovely little 2-bedroom terraced house. It needed some work doing on it, but Andy was brilliant with his hands and, in no time, had renovated it to a beautiful standard. 2 months later when he came home from work I gave him a little present. It was a box, the one from my Parker pen to be honest, but it was the content that was the best bit. Inside lay a plastic white stick with two little blue stripes in the window. Andy stared at it for ages, and then looked at me with tears in his eyes. 'Really?' he asked. 'Really' I answered, and he swung me up in the air and spun me round and then immediately put me down and faffed over me like a mother hen. 'I'm pregnant Andy, not dying!' I laughed. It was one of the best moments of our lives so far. 8 months later Molly arrived. A beautiful 7lb 3oz smushie faced beauty. We instantly fell in love with our angel. Life was perfect.

Well, until the late-night feeds, screaming and crying for no reason (and that was just me). As for the nappies,

I thought that to save money I would use terry nappies instead of the more modern disposable ones, which we couldn't afford to be honest. So, it was constant feeding, nappies, burping, soothing, teething, no sleep and do you know what? We wouldn't have changed a minute of it. Our perfect family.

18 months later we did it all again. Ellie was a tiny little 5lb 6oz angel, so delicate that we were frightened we'd break her. Thankfully we didn't, and she just added to the joy.

2 years later a little surprise arrived. This time with Billy who was a gorgeous chubby 8lb 7oz bundle of happiness. We had learned this time not to creep around the house on tip toes. We flushed the toilet at night. I hoovered around him during the day and he slept through the lot. Again, we were so happy. I loved being a mum so much. These three little beauties gave me so much love that I thought I would burst.

Sadly, our happiness was about to shatter. My dad Trevor was diagnosed with lung cancer. He had chemotherapy and radio therapy but there was nothing that could be done. The cancer had spread to his lymph nodes and his brain. He was told he had only a few months to live and Mum and I took it bad. This was my dad we were talking about. He didn't get sick. He was my hero who could do anything. If I had a problem, he would fix it. If I was sad he would cheer me up. I loved him so much and couldn't bear the fact that he wasn't going to be here much longer. We tried to give him everything he needed but he said that all he wanted was to walk me down the aisle.

We worked miracles and after speaking to our local vicar he agreed to give us a 'blessing'. We rallied round the family and my aunts, uncles and cousins helped with decorating the room and doing the buffet at the local labour club and Andy and I had enough savings for a wedding dress and suit hire.

Within 6 weeks my dad walked me down the aisle. I was mainly holding him up as he was exhausted, but we did it and we cried the whole time. In fact, most of us did. With all our red noses, the wedding pictures look like everyone is suffering from the flu.

Dad was in his wheelchair for most of the day and evening and needed his oxygen tank with him. It took a lot out of him to walk me down the aisle, but on top of that after Andy and I had done our first dance I felt a tap on my shoulder and turning around my dad asked if he could dance with me. The tears flowed as fast as the wine. This is something that will stay in my mind forever.

3 weeks later, with all of us around him, my wonderful dad passed away peacefully.

I was a wreck, but mum needed me, so I tried to be strong for her and my wonderful Andy was my lintel, holding me up whenever I thought I would crumble.

Mum stayed with us for a couple of months, which logistically wasn't easy as we only had a 2-bedroom house and 3 children, but we managed (pull out sofa beds may seem like a good idea but long term they're hell on your back). The kids were godsends as they carried on being happy and funny. Billy was just a baby, but Ellie and Molly could talk, and the hardest part was when they kept asking for grandad.

We tried to explain that he was now with the angels up in the sky and was always looking down on us, making sure we all stayed safe. Molly asked if he was with the angels helping to paint the sky blue, and now and again she would wave up at the sky, just in case he was watching.

I wanted to act on Dads advice, remembering all the things he had said about investments and buying and selling properties. After the insurance company paid out from dad's life insurance etc it turned out that Mum's mortgage was paid off and she had a healthy bank balance which meant she didn't have to worry about money any more. With his pension and that, mum could do whatever she wanted, but all she wanted was dad.

Eventually, she started to rebuild her life - which was such a relief as she went to a very dark place for a while, but she's now happily married to my step dad Mike and living in a beautiful cottage in Tenby. I don't get to see her as much as I would like to, and I know I'm going to have to bite the bullet and go and visit. It's just the thought of the twenty thousand questions that will be thrown at me, that puts me off. Selfish I know.

As for my wonderful dad, it also turned out that he'd left me a large sum of money. In fact, it was enough to buy a small plot of land and build 2 houses, which is exactly what we did. Andy was a fully trained City and Guild builder by now, so he did most of the work himself. Of his closest friends, one was an electrician and the other a plumber, which was very handy and fortuitous to say the least. I helped where I could, decorating and making the houses into homes. We sold them both before they were even finished and made quite a hefty profit. That was the start of Harper Builders Ltd, and within the first year the profits soared, and Harper Builders went from strength to strength.

I couldn't thank my dad enough. It's a devastating fact that we had to lose him to get our dream and it was a very bitter sweet thing indeed. It seems that Andy has forgotten all of that and I feel sad for him as those memories can't be replaced and neither should they. They make us who we are. I hope his young Aussie physio bitch is worth him forgetting all of this. Because now I'm angry, in fact I am fuming. He can go to hell and take his physio with him.

Chapter 5

Today I'm off on my holiday. The cottage I've booked is in a beautiful little town called Port Isaac, my dream property location and I am so excited. I've had enough gloom in the last few months to last a lifetime. So now it's me time. It's going to take at least 5 hours to drive there and I've just finished loading the car. It's going to be lovely having a total change of scenery.

It's 10.00 am now and I'm ready for the off. I've watered the plants and put them in a sink of water, put the radio on (why do we do that?), put the lamps on timer, set the alarm, locked the front door when the house phone rings. Bloody hell, that's typical. I unlock the door, disarm the alarm and answer the phone, but it's gone dead and the answer machine picks up.

'Hi Mum. It's just me, erm Molly.   I just wanted to say … erm … have a lovely trip and if you're passing anywhere near Bristol, come and see us. I miss you and I know the kids do too. Anyway erm, like I said I was just ringing to say have a … have a great time. Anyway, you've probably left already so you'll hear this when you come back. Ok, well that was all, nothing else. Love you. Erm ... Bye!'

Well, that was weird. Molly, never says I love you, like ever. She did seem a bit odd. Should I ring her back? No, be selfish. Ring when you arrive. Pretend you didn't get the message. Ooh that's devious but come on, this is the first/only holiday you've ever had on your own. Get your arse in gear and put the metal to the peddle or is it peddle to the metal? Erm you know something? I don't know but – get this – I don't care. I MANDY HARPER DON'T CARE!

I'm lying, I do care but I'm forcing myself to put me first. It isn't a natural thing for me to do, but I have to learn at some point so why not start now?

Feeling slightly anxious but fighting it I set the alarm again, lock the door and get into the car. I've prepped the car, done the tyres, filled the water thing with screen wash. Well I used fairy liquid instead but it's the same thing, isn't it? I wasn't sure how much to put in, so I put half a bottle. I hope that's enough. Anyway, I'm ready … again. The address is in the satnav and it says it'll take 5 hours and 8 minutes to get there. Right, off I go. Oh, damn it I need a wee now!

I unlock door, disarm alarm, pee, wash hands, set alarm, lock door, get in bloody car and just set off.

Admittedly I stall the first time in my haste to leave but now I'm on my way to sunny Cornwall.

I love it so much there. So many memories from spending our summer holidays there when I was a little girl. I never got to take the children as Andy preferred a holiday abroad. He said it never felt like a holiday if you stayed in the same country. He, and sadly they, missed out on a lot.

I've been driving for a couple of hours now and the journey has been beautiful. I had a bit of a hold up due to a car broken down in the middle lane, but the green hills make me feel calm. I've always loved driving, just never got the chance that often. If we went anywhere Andy would insist on driving so it just became automatic that I would go straight to the passenger side.

Anyway, I've got my music playing, please don't laugh, but it's Kenny Rogers – I love him. He is like a very sexy Santa which sounds weird I know, but still ... mmm, I wouldn't kick him out of bed. I would never have admitted that out loud before – and even though it's only me in the car, I'm still blushing.

My dad used to listen to him all the time and convinced me that in the song Lucille, the line 'with 4 hungry children and a crop in the field' was in fact 'with 400 children and a crap in the field'. I sang that for so many years. It still makes me smile when think of it.

I need a wee. Sorry to just blurt it out but I really do, and it's come on suddenly (I have had three children you know, and OK, maybe I didn't do enough pelvic floor exercises, but please don't judge) and it's all I can think of now. I'm looking for a sign with services written but none have come up yet, oh wait there's one - Services 21 miles. 21 MILES! I can't wait that long, not a chance. I'm going to have to go off one of the junctions and find a pub or supermarket or bush!

I come off at Walsall and luckily there is a B&Q. I run in and have a wee but feel guilty as though they all know that's all I came in for, so I start looking around for something cheap to buy and I settle on some wood screws. So, feeling happy and not guilty I pay the lovely chap in the orange overall called, and you'll never believe this, Kenny and I resume my journey to Cornwall doing pelvic floor exercises as I sing along to Lucille's crops.

I've been driving for another hour now and I'm getting a bit peckish. It's 1.00pm, so I pull into some services for a bite to eat and set off again. I'm in no rush at all. It's such an odd feeling not having someone else to think about. I don't have to worry about asking to stop at the next services for a wee or feel guilty for grabbing that family size bag of Maltesers for the journey (well there are only 11 calories in each one). But it is quite liberating. I'm feeling good, I mean really good and I'm only at the Gloucester services.

I've gone into the M&S store and grabbed a wrap, some fruit (healthy), a drink (and after a quick nip into the bit that sells everything from paracetamol to cuddly teddies), the Maltesers (not so healthy) and I'm off again; fed, watered and happy it only takes me another hour and a half until I see a sign for Taunton and it's only another hour or so from there.

According to the Port Isaac website "Port Isaac, was a busy coastal port from the Middle Ages to the mid-19th century when it was an active harbour where cargoes like stone, coal, timber and pottery were loaded and unloaded…. It's still used as a fishing harbour, but tourism plays an important part of economy." That's nice, but in all honesty, I'm just chuffed that I'm going where they film Doc Martin. If I'm lucky I might even get to see Martin Clunes.

After a couple of hours, the satnav takes me down a lovely little lane to the cottage and the view of the sea gives me butterflies in my stomach and tears in my eyes as I think back to my glorious childhood holidays. Although I haven't been to this area before it feels familiar and I love it already.

Audrey and Terry who own the cottage are waiting to greet me. They are a lovely couple, who welcome me instantly, as though we've been friends for years. They are a little surprised I've arrived on my own but cover it well.

'We've got you a few essentials in. Bread, milk and butter oh, and some tea and coffee.' Smiles Audrey. 'Terry will show you how everything works so you don't have to worry about anything. Also, we only live five minutes away, so I've left our address and telephone numbers on the kitchen table.' I thank them both for their hospitality and feel on cloud nine until innocently Terry asks when the others will be arriving. Ah …

I tell them it's just me and before I know what's happened Audrey has taken me under her wing. Within five minutes we are sat at the kitchen table while Audrey pours the tea out, and I pour my heart out. I'm so embarrassed but she's such lovely person and she is just so easy to talk to. I can imagine being friends with her for a long time. The minute the first tear rolled down my face Terry coughed, excusing himself saying he would bring my luggage in and went out to unload my car.

After another cup of tea, which Terry joined us for as I'd stopped crying like a baby, they said they'd leave me to get settled. At the door Audrey gave me a big hug and asked if I would like to come for dinner one evening. I accepted gladly. How lovely were these two strangers? I was truly touched. Terry dragged me into a one arm hug while patting my shoulder and said if I needed anything at all to just ring. I was totally humbled by this pair of strangers. They don't know me at all but treated me just like family. I already feel at home.

The cottage is gorgeous. Outside it's painted white with a lovely pastel blue front door surrounded by Jasmine, its scent wafting into the house with the slight breeze.

My home is a large five bedroom detached with two large gardens, and as I've mentioned before I love it because that's where our little family grew, but truthfully, it's huge with just me rambling around in it and the gardens are so big, that we've always employed gardeners to do everything (always to Andy's specifications). Although I love it dearly, and the thought of losing it breaks my heart, it doesn't seem quite so bad now I'm inside this quaint little cottage. Maybe this is just what I need. A fresh start, a new home? I don't need to think about that now, I just need to relax and enjoy the holiday.

Now I've stopped the waterworks and I'm left on my own I can see that the cottage is stunning inside and so cosy. The living room has a real open fire and there are logs in a basket at the side of the chimney breast. The walls are a pale cream and there are are a couple of two-seater sofas in tan leather and a coffee table with a vase with fresh flowers in. There are also a couple of side tables with lamps and a small tv. There is a doorway which leads to the back of the cottage with a kitchen diner that completes the whole back of the house. There are French doors which lead into the back garden which has a small patio and a small garden, with a cute little lawn surrounded by established bushes and some wild flowers. It's just perfect.

I take myself upstairs to check out the bedrooms. I know there are two and a bathroom up here. The doors all have garden latch handles and they're all just stained in their natural light oak colour. The first door on the left is a bedroom, it's small with a single bed but, if Chrissie decided to pop down for a couple of days, would be perfect for her. Next is the bathroom with a roll top bath, and telephone shower/taps and a sink and toilet. The walls are pale lemon and it is beautiful. I plan to make the most of this room. Note to self – buy bubble bath.

Finally, the last door. This is the master bedroom and although it's a lot smaller than my bedroom at home, is simply gorgeous. Its walls are the palest blue and the bedding is all crisp white with a navy throw on the bottom and a navy scatter cushion. There are two small light oak bedside tables with lamps and a wardrobe and set of drawers, but best of all is the view from the window facing the wrought iron bed. It's the sea. The sun is glinting off it and it looks amazing. The sun seems to be setting to the side of house, but you can see the pink glow in the sky and the reflection on the water. My cheeks are aching from smiling and I don't want to drag myself away from the window, but I've got all week to experience this, so I begin to unpack my case that Terry has kindly brought upstairs. It takes me no time to empty it, pop it under the bed and go downstairs to see what I can do for dinner.

By the kitchen is a typed booklet with instructions for the alarm, nearest doctors, shops and pubs and restaurants. It's now 6.30pm and I'm not sure if any of the shops will be open so I think I'll brave it and go for some dinner at the local pub which is only five minutes away. I grab my book - a favourite feel good book by Marian Keyes – and set off for my first solitary meal out. I can do this ...

No, I can't. I chicken out and go to the chippy for fish and chips. Not that it's a bad thing. I take it down to the beach and eat it there and just watch the waves crashing against the shore. It's after 9pm when I head back to the cottage. I would normally feel a little nervous walking alone at night but here doesn't seem to leave me with the same fear. The sound and scent of the ocean is truly calming.

I take a cup of tea up to bed and snuggle down for an early night. It's been a very long day, but I feel proud for organising all this myself and fall asleep with a smile on my face, which I haven't done for a very long time.

Chapter 6

I have slept with the bedroom window and curtains open and the early morning sunlight has burst into the room. I can hear the waves lapping on the shore and the view of the sea from the bed is stunning. Also, a huge bonus is that I slept right through. Which is amazing as with all the stress at home I hadn't had a full night sleep for ages. I haven't forgotten that behind the scenes the house is still being valued along with Andy's business and we've had to get transfer value figures from our pensions, up to date bank statements from personal to business accounts and wage slips etc for our financial disclosure. There's just so much to have to remember but being here has made it all easier to process, or at least put to the back of my mind. I just plan to make the most of this break. I'll deal with reality when I need to.

I go downstairs, put the kettle on and open the French doors. It's only 6.30 yet it's warm enough to have breakfast on the patio so that's exactly what I'm going to do. I make some tea and toast, grab my book and have the most peaceful and tasty breakfast I've had in a while. All this sea air is making me hungry.

Audrey and Terry have left me a map of the town and the date the market is on, which is the day after tomorrow. Even though it's Sunday she's written that most of the shops are open as it's the start of the tourist season. It'll be good to walk around the town in the day light and to see if anything has changed.

After a quick shower, I just blast my hair with the hairdryer, I normally take ages blow drying it to make it sleek and shiny how Andy liked it, but I have a natural wave to my hair, and no one here knows me, so I just tie it up in a loose bun, pop on a little makeup and SPF and go through my wardrobe to see what to wear. Being a size … erm 17, I am still limited and still have issues with my arms, so I go for my new jeans and a t-shirt. Fit flops in place and I'm off. I've read that these sandals tone while you walk, and I need all the help I can get. I'm hoping I'll have J-Lo's bum by the end of the week, but I think my expectations on this poor footwear may be a little high.

Port Isaac is simply stunning. I might buy myself some trainers or walking boots as the surrounding hills are gorgeous and I'll bet there are some amazing walks and views from up there. I might even do some drawing or painting, or photography – the realisation of just how much freedom I have literally fills me up and bursts through my fingers. I still miss Andy, I miss him so much that it hurts to think about him. It's almost like a bereavement, but there's also a new feeling, a good feeling, but I can't quite put my finger on what it is, or even how to describe it. I'm sure it will come to me but right now I'm just happy to watch the people on the beach laughing and loving life. There's quite a few now and more are arriving as I look. I see now what's going on, it seems that the area is a favourite for surfers as I watch them put on wetsuits and get their boards ready. What surprises me most is the quantity of women there. I'm not sure why I always thought it would be a man's sport but obviously I am totally wrong as there are equal numbers of men and women.

Near here are the beautiful towns of Tintagel, Boscastle and Crackington Haven. Mum and Dad used to bring me here on our summer holidays. It has a huge sandy beach which is 3-mile-long and as a small child it looked like it went on forever and ever. Just thinking about it makes my tummy tingle and my eyes tear up. Dad might not be here anymore, but his memories live on and I can picture him burying me in the sand or making me a huge sand car to sit in. I'm so lucky to have parents who loved me so very much. All our holidays were centred around me and as an only child that obviously meant they had to play all the games with me as I had no sibling to play with, although I did manage to make friends every year with other children on holiday.

With that lovely memory inside me, making me smile, I go for a walk into the town thinking how lovely it will be to bring mum back here. I think she'll like it just as much as I do. I love it here and instantly feel at home and more importantly, at peace.

In the town itself there's mainly one street with shops on and few off shoots with tourist shops, selling candles, shells and even starfish. But, I don't need those. What I do need is to stock up on some food for dinners, as to be honest it will be lovely to just sit in the garden having my meals and watching the sun set over the Atlantic.

I call into the butchers and a cheery chubby man appears from behind the plastic curtains.

'Alright, my dear, what can I do you for?' His smile is infectious, so smiling back I order my food, a chicken breast and a lovely bit of sirloin steak.

'Just for one of you, then is it?' he enquires looking innocent. It prickles a little, but his face looks so earnest that I can't take offence.

'Yes, just the one', I say trying my best to sound friendly. He asks if I'm staying at Audrey and Terry's house and I confirm that yes, I am.

'Oh, you're the poor woman whose hubby's run off with that 'Young bloody Aussie Physio who spells her name funny' aren't you?' I stare at him in shock. How presumptuous! How rude! How dare Audrey spread this gossip about me.

'These are on the house my love, and I've thrown you in a couple of sausages too. All I can say is what an idiot to walk out on a lovely lass like you.' He blushes as he says it and all my fury and indignation melts away. This man, who doesn't know me at all – although clearly knows more about me than I would have liked – has shown kindness and compassion and he's not judging me or even making me feel embarrassed. On the contrary, I feel like I could give him a hug for being so lovely. But, as his apron is covered in blood I think I'll just say thank you and bye.

Just as I'm walking out the door, still thanking him, he says 'Oh, there's a pub quiz on Wednesday night if you … erm … if you fancy it?' He's blushing a little and rubs the back of his neck with his hand. 'Our team is a bit short and we could do with an extra brain. It's the Dog and Duck, just down the road here and it starts at 8.00. So, I'll see you then.' It wasn't really a question but, I laugh and agree. Why the hell not?

I get home, well I mean back at the cottage, a few hours later and am feeling quite peculiar. Other than my new walking trainers I have not spent any money on food and I've been into the Bakers, Fruit and Veg shop and Fishmongers. I've not even been here one day, and everyone knows me. I know news travels fast in small towns, but this has put Fibre Broadband to shame.

It's only Sunday and I have plans for dinner with Audrey and Terry, quiz night with John (Butcher) on Wednesday, I'm going to a salsa class on Tuesday with Mary (Bakery) and Karaoke (I cringe) with Tina (Fishmonger) and Kay (Fruit and Veg) on Thursday. I'm not sure a week stay is long enough. Chrissie and the kids will never believe me when I tell them how much my social life has improved.

These people are so adorable. They have all opened themselves to me and invited me, a stranger, into their lives. Wow … just wow.

I had a nagging feeling when I thought about the kids and I can't rememb ... Oh no, I do remember. Molly left me that weird message and now I'm going to have to pretend I didn't get it. I feel so bad I ring her straight away, but it goes to answer machine, so I leave a message asking her to ring me. I do hope she's OK. I'll call in to see them on the way home and maybe even stay a day or two. They could have a night out without the kids and it'll be so nice to see the twins, plus I haven't any clients until the end of next week, so I should be OK.

I make myself a sandwich and a cup of tea and take it outside onto the patio, which I'm guessing will soon become the only place I eat or drink anything.

Birds are singing, bees are buzzing, waves are crashing, and I can hear laughter and music in the distance. I wish I could record the sound as it instantly soothes and calms even though I haven't felt that worked up. In fact, I've hardly thought about Andy all day, until now when I'm talking about not thinking about him (mental eye roll). This place must be good for me.

Tucking into my ham and tomato sandwich on the freshest bread I've 'never' bought, and my phone rings. It's Molly returning my call. Act cool.

'Hi love, how's everything going? Is Charles busy at work? How are the kids? I'll bet they're a handful?' (and breath) God forbid I should overdo it.

'Fine, fine.' She obviously lies back. I can't say anything as she'll know I was a horrible mother by not speaking to her the other day. What do I do?

'How are the children?' I ask again.

'Fine, fine.' She answers.

'Erm and Charles? How's he?' I repeat, like a parrot (this is like pulling teeth).

'Fine, yes he's fine.' She answers again. I'm hoping her vocabulary improves or this is going to be a very long, monosyllabic conversation.

'Well, this place is amazing honey.' I think a change of topic might gee her up a little. 'It's beautiful. We'll have to come here together with the children and Charles. There's a lovely beach and some walks to go on....' I trail off as I'm running out of things to say. Oh, bugger it. I'm going in and hopefully I'll come out undamaged.

'Molly, are you OK love? You don't sound yourself.' I use my marvellous mother's intuition skills. She'll know all about those.

Then the unexpected happens, Molly, my strong independent Molly, bursts into tears. I'm not used to this as I'm the emotional one, not her. I cry at everything. Including the old Gillette adverts with the father and son's shaving (I'm filling up just thinking about it). I don't know what to do. I try to speak platitudes of which I'm ashamed, as they do nothing to sooth or calm her. I may as well be there patting her on the back from six feet away with a broom handle whilst mumbling 'there, there'.

Thankfully, she stops crying. 'I'm OK now mum. I just needed to (sniff, sniff) let it (sniff, sniff) out.'

'Do you want to talk about it? It can help if you talk...' I don't get to finish as she simply blurts out.

'It's about Dad.' (Oh God, don't tell me now. I'm on holiday. My cup of tea is evaporating in the heat and flies are enjoying the remainder of my sandwich.)

'Is he OK?' Hopefully, she's ringing to tell me that he can't stand living with the physio anymore as she's constantly having a go at his posture and wants to apologise and get back together so at least he can slouch again. But no, it's not that …

'He's moved in with Zooey,' (which I knew) 'and they're planning to move to Australia when the divorce becomes final.' (Which I did not know). She waits for me to speak but I have no words, or rather I have lots of words but they're all in my head, muddled up, fighting to come out of my mouth.

Molly tries again. 'Mum? Are you still there? I think I've lost signal. Mum? Hello? Are you OK?'

'Sorry love, I'm fine. It was just a bit of a shock.' I reply.

'Oh, I'm so sorry to have just blurted it out. I wasn't very tactful, was I? I'm so sorry mum.' I can tell she's mortified, all the 'sorry's' are a sign, but her voice is breaking as she's talking. This must be hard for her, so I 'mum up' and with as strong a voice as I can use (which I think would make Emily Pankhurst proud) I say.

'Fuck him!'

Obviously, Molly is not used to her PC mum using foul language, and swearing is a sign of poor language skills, but right now those were the only ones to make their way to my mouth. We are both stunned into silence and then I start laughing as I'm as shocked as she is and that sets her off laughing. Before we know it, we are both howling with laughter down the phone. My belly is aching so much and when I can form a coherent sentence I tell her that I'm going to call and stay for a day or two at the end of the week if that's ok. Molly's thrilled and laughing, we say our goodbyes.

I put the phone back on the table and burst into tears.

Chapter 7

The news that Andy is planning on moving to Australia hits me hard. After my phone call with Molly I just broke down. I'm not sure that it had really sunk in until that point. Even though I was furious that he would throw away over 30 years of what we had built up, a wonderful family and successful business, I am embarrassed to admit that I would have taken him back in a flash. But something has changed. Whether it was because he'd told Molly first with no thought to either, a) her feelings, b) mine, or the fact that he has just done the whole thing with no thought for any of us, has made my blood boil. I need to speak to Ellie and Billy as I don't even know if they've been told.

Obviously, Andy was feeling in a rut, but don't we all feel that? Middle age was creeping up and he was starting to look older and we definitely all feel that! A young Australian Physiotherapist has thrown herself lustily (is that a word?) at him and it's made him feel younger. Wouldn't we all like to feel younger? I'm not saying that you should jump into bed and leave your wife/husband/kids for a younger person, but of course it would be flattering to be hit on. FLA-TTER-ING. End of! A boost to your confidence, a realisation that you still have it, but wouldn't dream of acting on it, NOT an actual reason to break up a long-term relationship and throw away memories as easily as emptying the bin. I can hear it now, "When you put the bins out can you remember to put the memory bin with the blue and green ones this week love?" No, you do not throw all that away like it's nothing, and to top it off he's made my tough daughter, who didn't even cry watching The Green mile, cry. So, now I'm fuming. Really, fucking fuming. (I've said that twice now, Chrissie will be so proud of me).

By the time I've stopped crying/fuming/ranting etc the sun is setting. I don't want to cook anything, so I just make a cup of tea and a sandwich (the flies are not having any this time) and sit and watch the sunset, comforted by my book and a bar of fruit and nut (some things never change).

I must have nodded off as I wake, chilly now, to the phone ringing. It's Chrissie. A huge smile comes on my face as I've missed her, especially today. I'd normally turn to her and her to me when any crisis comes along but I knew she was busy today with a family christening and I didn't want to mither her.

'Hi honey!' I say answering the phone, happy to hear her voice even though it's only been a couple of days since I saw her. 'How was the Christening?'

'Dull, long and fuckin' infuriating! How are the cider loving, cream tea loving folks of the west country treating you?' She sounds like she's forcing herself to be happy.

'The people here are amazing!' I go into the story of what's happened from meeting Audrey and Terry to the kind people in the village giving me food via Port Isaac's very own Fibre Broadband. I then tell her about my phone call with Molly.

'He's what?' she shrieks so loud down the phone that I think she's possibly given me tinnitus. 'What a fucking prick! And a coward!' Not one to mince her words Chrissie continues her tirade. 'Telling his daughter first? I didn't think he could stoop any lower, but the man has outdone himself. He knew she'd have to tell you and I know you were being a saddo and thinking things would work out AND you'd take him back if he came, but please tell me that is not what's going on in your head now?' She's livid, not surprisingly so and if anyone other than family has my back it's Chrissie. I love this woman like a sister and I know she feels the same. So, I'm quite excited to tell her what I said when Molly told me.

'No! You are not telling me that Amanda Harper cussed out loud. You actually used the 'f word'?' she whispers the last bit and then bursts out laughing.

'I did, and it felt good.' I laugh with her. 'Obviously, this hasn't changed me into the kind of woman whose language would make a builder blush, but words had escaped me and those two hadn't.'

'I'm so proud of you.' She says as she sniffs an imaginary tear and I tell her to bugger off. Then I remember what she'd said about the Christening.

'Anyway, moving on, why was the Christening infuriating? I know they can be boring as hell, especially when there's loads of babies being done at the same time and they can drag on a bit, but what made it so bad?'

Chrissie then tells me about this gorgeous guy she met who was from her cousin's husbands side and he came over and said hello. Anyway, this fella, who is quite attractive for an arsehole (her words, not mine) gets into a conversation with her and it's going quite well, they've had a few glasses of wine, and are chatting about all kinds of stuff - weather, jobs (he's an accountant, yawn) countries they've been to and would like to go to and they seem to have a lot in common. That is until the subject of marriage comes up. He's never been married as he's never met the right person and there are so many divorces these days that he says it's put him off.

'Do you know what he fuckin' said then? Do you?' she asks rhetorically, as I feel the heat of her fury coming off her down the phone and know better than to butt in when she's in full-on rant mode. 'He said that he'd heard about someone in the family who compounded his argument for not getting married. Some gold digger who'd been married five times and it was women like her that put him right off.' She takes a breath and I take a drink (I'd made myself a brew and got the biscuits out during her rant as this was definitely one of those chats). Chrissie continues.

'Is that right? I say to him. Do you know the woman you're talking about? Do you know the circumstances of

64

any of it? Well he's starting to sweat a little at this point as I think he knows he's cocked up *big time*.'

'What happened then?' I mumble with a mouth full of biscuit, although I needn't have bothered as Chrissie is ploughing on regardless.

'But no, he was just sweating because he was warm, and he carried on oblivious of my obvious anger. He said her name was something like Kirsty or Christine or something and he bet she was some blonde bimbo with cosmetically enhanced parts and a face full of Botox who lured in these sad saps and then went off with their money!' All I could do was eat my biscuits and drink my tea.

'Oh, sweetheart what an absolute horror of a man! I hope you gave it to him! What did you do?'

'Nothing.'

'What? Say that again, I think I'm losing signal or something.' I am absolutely flabbergasted. I mean I've obviously misheard. The Chrissie I know would have told him where to go stick his opinion and I believe it's somewhere the sun doesn't shine.

'I did nothing.' She repeats, and sounds upset. 'At that moment, my cousin Helen came over shouting, "Chrissie, that's where you are, Auntie Mary wants to see you." I looked back at Simon and he's gone white as he realises that I'm the "cosmetically enhanced" gold digger. So, as I left to go with Helen I turned back and said, 'It's three actually, not five'.

She said that he just looked crushed and apologetic, but she was being dragged off by Helen and the next time she looked he was walking out the door.

'Do you know the worst part Mandy? I liked him. I really liked him. I'm not saying you had to get your big wedding hat out of the box, but we got on so well and were laughing and we talked none stop. Is that what people think of me? That I'm just a gold digger? Do Helen's out-laws think of me as a joke? Let's all laugh at Chrissie. I'd laugh myself if it wasn't so tragic. You know I didn't get a penny. I didn't want one, that's not who I am and that's not who I wanted this guy to think I was. I wouldn't mind but I hadn't felt this comfortable with anyone in a long time.' She takes a breath and I can hear she's having a drink as I hear the ice chink in the glass. This isn't Chrissie. She's a fighter. She doesn't care what people think. I need to use my best counselling skills to help my best friend. And so, after taking a deep breath I say …

'Fuck him!'

Chapter 8

I t's Monday morning and I'm exhausted. My conversation with Chrissie has left me unsettled. Her reaction to this guy is so unlike her and I didn't sleep well for worrying. Normally she would just tell him to mind his own business and to sod off, not that should would have put it quite as mildly as I have. He obviously got under her skin and therefore has got under mine. I'll ring her tonight as she'll be at work all day.

We work at a hospice called Shire Bank. It's a beautiful Georgian building that used to belong to Lord Fauntleroy or something and is set in the middle of a landscaped garden with a willow tree in the centre hanging over a pond filled with Koi carp. You can just sit out there on the benches and listen to the birds and watch the fish. It really is the most tranquil setting for everyone, carers and patients alike and especially lovely for those nearing the end of life. It just gives you a feeling of peace and tranquillity and hopefully today during Chrissie's lunch break it will bring her some of that. I hate to think of her doubting herself.

After breakfast, I shower and pack up a small picnic as today I'm going to take my new trainers for a walk. I throw my drawing pad and pencils in my rucksack just in case and set off. Look at me, Amanda Harper, walking! I know that sounds a bit pathetic but I'm not the energetic type. Don't get me wrong I'm not lazy, I just don't exercise. It's like a dirty word that brings me out in a sweat, but I guess that's the point. Running is what water does, not me. The thought of running through the streets while my flab is jiggling along with me is enough to give me palpitations and it's pretty much the same at a gym, the only difference is I'm trapped in a gym and it's the same people watching me jiggle, AND to top it off the rooms are full of mirrors so then I have no choice but to watch my own flab jiggle! I shudder at the thought. No, exercise and I don't mix well.

Anyway, that aside I have put my mind to spending my day walking along the coastal path and I set off with gusto.

The view of the sea, beach and cliffs is beautiful, and seeing the town with its eclectic mix of pastel coloured houses, all different shapes and sizes from this position is wonderful. Not something I would have seen from the car.

It's so lovely and calm and I can't remember the last time I was this relaxed. Andy should see this place, I do think he'd love it. Oh great, why did I have to think of him? I've totally ruined the calm and joy of my trip and

I've only been out a couple of hours. Wow, I've been walking for 2 hours and although I'm sweating buckets and possibly dehydrated because of it, I'm also grateful for the fact that I've not had a cardiac arrest. I decide to turn back as it's going to take me the same amount of time to get back, but this time I walk back on the beach.

Collapsing, rather than sitting on a sand dune (I have been walking for a whole morning you know) I watch families playing with their children and people walking their dogs. There are a few people surfing but it looks like they're just learning on the gentle waves. I briefly wonder whether I could do something like that, but only briefly as I realise the fright I'd look being squeezed into one of those wetsuits (black pudding comes to mind).

I take my picnic from my bag and start to eat when I see my pad and pencils. Why not, I think. No one is here to judge me, in fact no one even needs see them as I'm doing this just for me.

I'm surprised at how comfortable I feel drawing and my attempt isn't half bad. I've finished my lunch and am just about to pack everything up when a dog comes bounding around the corner of the dune straight into me. He then stops and sits with his tail wagging.

'Why hello….' I check his dog tag 'Scruff.' I laugh as he's just panting and wagging. He's a gorgeous sandy coloured dog, about the size of a small Labrador with little tufts of fur that stand up. I'm not quite sure on the breed (possibly a Heinz 57) but he's adorable and so well behaved, if you forgo the fact that he's obviously just run away from his owner.

'Scruff! Here boy!' I hear a man's voice and obviously so does Scruff. His ears prick up and he's off running towards the voice of whom I'm guessing belongs to his owner.

'Come on now, back on the lead.' The voice sounds oddly familiar but as I know no one down here (and it wasn't a Cornish accent) it's obvious that he probably just sounds like someone I know.

I gather my things together and put them back in my rucksack and by the time I've walked around the sand dune, Scruff and his owner have gone. I head back home and realise I've been out for over 5 hours. 5 hours, just walking and drawing. Ha! Wait until I tell Chrissie, she'll never believe me.

My feet, knees and back are aching by the time I get back from my walk and I think my blisters have blisters, but even though I'm sore, I'm proud that I walked so far, and surprised that I actually enjoyed it. I make myself a cuppa and ring Ellie and Billy. I'm not sure if they know what their dad is doing but if not, one of us should tell them and it shouldn't have to be their big sister.

I ring Ellie first. 'Hi Mum, how's the holiday?' she sounds upbeat, so I assume she hasn't been told. How do I break this awful news to her? I know she's not a little girl anymore but still, it's going to upset her.

'The place is gorgeous sweetie, but I need to talk to you first.' I feel emotional just knowing that she's going to be crushed.

'Is it about Dad moving?' She asks with an ease that is surprising to say the least.

'Erm ... yes love, but its where he's moving to that I'm ringing you about.'

'Australia.' She cuts in.

It turns out that my beautiful, brave daughter Molly has told all of them as she thought I was going through enough as it is. It fills my heart with a mixture of pride, sadness and fury. I'm so proud of Molly, of the woman she's become, but also of how much she wanted to protect me. I'm so sad that things have come to this with Andy and that he has let them down more than me. But, as for fury ... I am livid, in fact I'm beyond livid, I'm bloody nuclear. How could he? He put all this pressure on poor Molly, without a thought for her, Ellie or Billy. What an absolute coward.

We've seen friends go through divorces where the adults change into unrecognisable people filled with bitterness and anger and we always said how bad it was that they couldn't go through it amicably.

I refuse to sink to his level. I'm not going to ring and shout and scream. I'm going to do 4 things.

1. Ring Billy
2. Put the kettle on
3. Grab the McVities
4. Ring Chrissie

I ring Billy but doubt he'll answer as he's probably in a lecture. If he is, I'll leave a message and get him to ...

'Hi mum!' he answers sounding chirpy.

'Oh, erm hi love, I wasn't sure you'd be in a lecture.'

'Just on a break, so free to chat to my favourite mum.' He laughs.

'*Favourite* mum? Cheeky.'

'How's the holiday?'

'It's great love and I'm having a lovely time thanks. Listen, I'm sorry to go straight into this but I know Molly has told you about dad and I wanted to check you were OK. I would have told you myself, but poor Molly was the one to tell me in the first place. I'm so sorry love.'

'Why are you sorry? You've done nothing wrong mum, it's dad that's being an arse, and I'm putting it politely.' I go to reprimand him for swearing about his dad, but why should I? He's an adult and is acting more mature than his father is.

It turns out that Molly was so worried about me and wanted to make it easier for me, so she told Ellie and Billy first. That way they wouldn't be too shocked when I rang them to tell them, which obviously she knew I'd do. God bless my level-headed girl.

'I was going to ring you tonight mum to see how you were, but you beat me to it. I knew something was going to happen, although I admit it was a shock hearing he's moving to the other side of the world.' I can hear the upset in his voice and know he feels as let down by his dad as I do, but he's putting on a brave face and I'm proud of him for it.

'Are you ok though Billy?'

'To be honest mum it's probably the best thing for you.' Eh? What is he talking about? I am so shocked by this comment that I'm lost for words.

'Dad has always just done stuff his way and you've always had to just follow. He was always out on some business dinner or other and you were left at home with us and a house to sort out. It was the same with our holidays. In the end I don't know why he ever came.' It seems Billy isn't lost for words.

'I … erm … I don't know what to say love. I didn't know you felt like this. Why didn't you ever talk to me?' *Did they all feel the same way?* 'But please let me make something very clear, from the minute you were born I have loved every minute of looking after you three, even the teenage years, and it was never a chore. You're my life. All of you.' I'm on the verge of the floodgates opening again. I can't believe that my children understood the dynamics of mine and Andy's relationship better than I did. Have I been kidding myself all these years that I had the perfect marriage? The perfect husband?

'I know mum,' he sounds choked up and all I want to do is wrap my arms around him and make his pain go away. If Andy were here now I think I'd throttle him. 'I didn't say anything mum because it's your life, not ours and if you were happy then so were we. We had a fab childhood, don't think that we didn't. It's just that as we got older, Dad seemed to become more interested in the business than in us.'

Billy, my loving son has kept this bottled up for all these years. No wonder he moved so far away to university and what kind of counsellor am I if I haven't even recognised these emotions in my own children.

'You must have thought me such a fool?' I whisper, emotion taking hold of my vocal chords.

'Why? For making a happy home for us? There's nothing foolish about that.' Gosh, my son has grown into a very sensible young man.

We talk for another half an hour. Billy tells me all about University and his upcoming exams. I bring up the subject of the house, not our home anymore, just the house and he said it won't be easy saying goodbye to the place but wherever I am will be home. We hang up and I promise to ring when I get home from my holiday.

I come off the phone and before I can get to step 2 on my list, I burst into tears (for a change).

Chapter 9

It's Tuesday evening and I'm getting ready for Salsa class. I must admit I'm aching in places I didn't know could ache from all the walking I've been doing, and I've got a bit of a golden glow from the lovely weather, but I'm really looking forward to tonight. I used to love dancing and I can't remember the last time I danced. I hope my 2 left feet remember which way to go.

I have decided to wear one of my new dresses. It's a gorgeous body con dress which is black with huge cerise pink orchids down one side and it has sleeves to the elbow and a small v-cut at the front which shows a little cleavage. I'm not sure it's the sexy salsa look but I feel great, so I don't care. I don't have a pair of dance shoes, but Mary has a spare pair which she said I can borrow.

I've curled my hair and put a little extra makeup on which makes me feel even better and if Chrissie could see me now she wouldn't believe it. I admit I had gotten into a rut with Andy, but I've pulled myself out of it, or maybe been dragged, either way I'm here and I feel good. And I didn't have to run off with a 'Young bloody Australian Physiotherapist who can't spell her name right!' (and relax)

I have no idea what to expect at the Salsa class but it's nothing like I imagined it would be. I think I expected lots of gorgeous Spanish looking couples dressed in exotic, sexy outfits with the men wearing all black, with slicked back hair … I'd obviously given it some thought. Imagine my surprise when I get there. For a start, the age range is from mid-30's up to late 70's, how on earth are older dancers going to keep up with the fast tempo of the Salsa? Also, there are more people here wearing cardigans than at an M&S winter sale. I feel quite young and sprightly even if I have two left feet. If I get to dance with someone who has two right feet, I'll be OK.

The dance tutor is super tanned, with a full head of black hair, which if I'm not mistaken is from a bottle, and he is totally hilarious and called Julio (turns out his name is Tony and he's a local mechanic but likes to act the part, terrible accent included) and I love him already.

Julio claps his hands and shouts 'Heveryone, we hev a new preety lady to our leetle salsa class so let's make her feel welcome!'. (I told you his accent was terrible.) Everyone claps and I'm blushing so much that I'm sure people can feel the heat coming off me. It's worse than slimming class where everyone claps if you so much as fart.

I'm still trying not to laugh at the fact that 'Julio' has the worse Spanish/Cuban accent I have ever heard, and his lips are making their way from my hand to my elbow. Normally I would cringe at his insistence of kissing my hand/arm, but in this environment, he's harmless and regardless of blushing, I can't wipe the smile off my face.

'Hokay, peepul grab a dance partner and L-e-et's Salsaaaaa.' He claps his hands, and everyone grabs a partner. I am the only one left, ironically partner-less again it seems, but Julio comes to the rescue and grabs hold of my waist and pulls me to him. Oh god, what have I let myself in for?

The following two hours are the most fun I've had in ages. I have mamboed and cha cha cha'd my bum off and it was fantastic! I started off dancing with Tony, oops I mean Julio and ended up dancing with everyone, one time with a lady who must have been at least 70, but boy was she nimble. Mary and I get together at the end.

'Did you have fun?' she asks.

'Fun? Mary, I can't thank you enough for the invite. I've had an amazing night and it's all thanks to you.' I decide there and then that on my last night, Friday, I'm going to have a little party at the house and invite a few special people and would Mary like to come. She blushes with delight and agrees. I must remember to speak to Audrey and Terry and ask if they would mind coming to mine for dinner instead of the other way around. I mean, if it wasn't for their gossiping I would never have met such wonderful people.

We part ways and I thank Julio for a great night. He's sad to hear that I'm only there for one night and I admit so am I. I know I'm only here for a week, but I've loved every bit of it so far and I've only been here for a few days. It's making me think about my future, but I don't want to rush into making any decisions just yet.

I ring Chrissie on the way home and we laugh together at how funny Julio was and she agrees he sounds adorable. What she can't believe is how adventurous I've been, and to be honest neither can I. If you'd told me 6 months ago that I would be walking hills and going to a Salsa class, I would have laughed my head off. My comfort zone is spreading and I'm happy to allow the changes.

I know I keep saying it, but I love it here and it's awful to think that after this week I won't see any of these wonderful people again. It's a sobering thought but I brush it aside and focus on the positives.

I ask Chrissie if she's heard any more from that horrible guy 'Simon' and she says that to be honest she's avoided all her family and deleted any voice mails from them without listening first.

'Why?' I ask her shocked, as she is the last person I ever thought would hide from anything or anyone.

'I can't get out of my head what they're all saying about me. Someone obviously had a good old laugh at me to Helen's in-laws, and it's the fact that there are people out there who know things about me and I don't have a clue who they are. I could have been talking to them and inside they would have been just laughing at me. It's stuck in my head Mand, all these lies, and I can't get it out of there.'

I can't believe what I'm hearing from my friend. She sounds so deflated. Her no-nonsense attitude normally has me wishing I could be more like that, but it seems that the roles are reversed, and she's turned into me and I into her and I would never wish that on anyone, especially my amazing friend.

'Oh, Chrissie love, who cares what anyone thinks? You know the truth about your marriages and divorces and whether you'd been married three times, seven times or bloody nine times, it's no one's business but yours and your ex's. Some people are so narrow minded and just love to judge. I'll bet their lives aren't perfect and people in glass houses shouldn't throw stones.' I take a breath and then say, in my sternest voice. 'Don't make me swear again Mandy, twice in one week is quite enough.'

At least I make her laugh a little, but I can still hear she's upset.

'Hey, I know, why don't you come down on the train and stay here with me. I have a spare room with your name on it!'

'I can't love, I have a busy week at work.' She sounds like she needs the opposite and a few days of Cornish air would do her good. Hmm, I'll have a think about what I can do to make her come down here, but for now we'll just have to chat on the phone.

We finish the call with us promising to go out together somewhere on Sunday. I love this woman like a sister and I hate to think of her sat alone trying to justify her life to herself. If I could get my hands on that man I'd throttle him and give him a piece of my mind.

I arrive home around 10.00pm. Home. It's funny to call it that but it feels right to say it.

I can't believe how much my hips are aching already from all the walking I've been doing and the cha cha cha-ing tonight.

I have a quick shower, stick my pj's on, make a cuppa and snuggle down in bed to read my book. I've checked the weather report for tomorrow and it says it's going to rain so I've decided I'm going to drive out to Tintagel and Boscastle for a spot of reminiscing.

I'm thoroughly exhausted and can't keep my eyes open so I switch off my light and nod off into a lovely deep sleep.

I dream I'm dancing and twirling, round and round and one minute I'm with George Clooney, then Julio, finally with Andy but as he twirls me he fades away and I can't see his face and then he's gone …

Chapter 10

It's Wednesday and quiz night tonight. The weather today is gloomy, a little like my mood, and it's pouring with rain. I think that I might just spend a bit of time at the cottage and catch up on my reading. I also know that I should work out what I'm going to do when I get home, and truthfully, I'm scared to death. This last few days has been an escape and I know I've been in a bit of denial over what's happened.

When I think of Andy leaving me I feel an enormous wave of panic start – what am I going to do? Where am I going to live? Why would he sleep with someone else? Sex, it's the most intimate thing you can do between two people, at least in my mind, and I can't get over the fact that he's intimately touched another woman and she's touched him too. Awful thoughts of them naked together are crushing me and the fact that she's twenty years younger than me, well I'm sure you can imagine where my thoughts are going. I've had three kids, I have stretchmarks and breasts that only see north if I stand on my head! That aside, he threw away everything we had built up over the last 33 years and I can't even ask him why because he's ignoring my calls. Yes, I've called him, and I'm ashamed to say I've left messages begging him to come home. All for nothing as he's still not told me properly why he left.

I think that's the biggest question that has been going around my mind. Why? I thought we had a good marriage. OK, we married young, but we were in love, weren't we? Had I changed? I know I'd put weight on over the years and my bingo wings could do their own round of applause when I waved, but Andy was no Arnie. I loved him, and we were happy, or rather I thought we were happy. When you grow together you sort of expect that you'll both grow *old* together, your bodies changing together, that's just how it should be. You don't really question it, not really. I mean some of my friends would talk about their husbands taking them for meals or romantic little breaks in a log cabin, complete with hot tub. Andy's usual reply to that would be, 'Why the hell would I want to stay in a shed and have a bath outside? You must be joking love!' and that would be the end of that discussion.

Even though I can't forget, I really do try not to think about the whole issue of him having sex with someone else, or eventually me having sex with someone else. Oh God, I'll have to keep shaving my legs again or having them waxed and having a Brazilian or a Hollywood, whatever the hell that is. I've had sex with one person in my whole life. One! I'm not naïve or anything, I've read Fifty Shades of Grey. The fact that I went fifty shades of red is irrelevant. The thing is you get comfortable with what you know and bearing in mind we didn't know much when we first got together, we've just learnt as we went along.

As a joke I bought Andy the Kamasutra for our 10th Wedding anniversary. It was fun at first, but he pulled his back doing The Plow, so we didn't bother with any more.

We are taught from a young age that we will all find 'The One', our knight in shining armour, our one true love. TV programmes, films, books, magazines, fairy tales – all had that thing in common. 'The One'. Maybe the latter one was the right one and it was just a fairy tale, but it's always said with such feeling and confidence, like it's some pre-destined path that we all take, and fate or destiny will all play a part in finding that one person in billions. The question that's been on my mind lately is, are there more than one 'The One's' if it turns out the first one isn't the right one? (Blimey, that's a mouthful.)

What happens when the one you think is it, walks out after 33 years? Are you doomed to being single forever? Don't get me wrong, although I can't imagine being with another man right now, I'm not daft, I know people get over these things and there is a light at the end of the tunnel. The thing is, what happens if I meet someone, who I'm attracted to and he likes me and there's a spark? Do I know what a spark is?

When Andy asked me out it was a definite yes. Was there a spark? I know I fancied him and he seemed to like me (I never quite understood that bit) but a spark? I don't even know.

I think by now you understand that I've never been overflowing with confidence. Some girls at my school would eat mars bars for breakfast, chips and gravy for lunch, with some more chocolate or something high in calories for pudding and were so skinny and had so much confidence that if they bottled it and sold it they would have been millionaires. Believe me I would have been first in the queue to buy some. As you can gather, I wasn't one of them. I wasn't obese or anything, I just wasn't skinny. I was slim and curvy and to be honest that's the last thing you want aged 14, or at least that's how it was then. Now all the girls want to look like one of the Kardashians.

Even as a young woman I wasn't much better. I'm sure you've been there, you're ready for a night out, make up done, hair done, you still don't feel 100% but hope that your clothes will make you feel good. Three outfits later, mascara down your face (waterproof mascara is a con) and you sit there crying, until your hubby comes in and says, 'Just bloody pick something will you!' or was that just me?

Anyway, back to Andy asking me out. It was a no brainer, of course I said yes, hell yes! I was so amazed that a boy this cool fancied me that I was … well grateful, for want of a better word.

It's sort of been like that all through our marriage. Please don't get me wrong we were in love and had a good marriage. I just wish I had some backbone. Andy made all the decisions and I let him. Should I have spoken up and said what I'd prefer? Could I have had an opinion? I mean, holidays always abroad and never in England (I did try hard with that one, but it was always a simple no.)

It was the same when we bought our home. It was a large 5-bedroom house which needed completely renovating. Oh, I was so excited. I could imagine a distressed farmhouse kitchen being the heart of the house, drawing everyone there whether they were friends, family or the kids, and we would obviously keep all original features, roll top bath, open staircase with oak newel post and spindles ... I had so many ideas for it.

Anyway, I'm getting carried away. I lost that argument too. Andy wanted modern, saying it would add value and what did I know? I wasn't a property developer, I was just a young mum. He even got a landscape gardener in, ensuring that I wasn't allowed to do the garden. The bigger his business got, the bigger his ego got and the more it all became about image with him. When I think about it, the longer we were married the more lost I became. Maybe we didn't have such a good marriage after all.

Another example - I would never, *ever*, have dreamt of booking a holiday for just Andy and me, let alone just for me. Andy booked all the holidays, even after the kids left home and it was just the two of us. He would naturally head for his English sports bar, and I would stay nearby, just reading, not exploring or drawing or do anything for just me. And now look at me. I've booked a holiday, in England! I know that Chrissie was there reassuring me, but it wasn't just her encouragement that made me do it, although it did help, but I just thought why not? You can do whatever you want, and Cornwall was the first thing I wanted, maybe next time I'll go further afield. I've always wanted to go to Barcelona, but Andy wouldn't go there as he thought it would be too trendy and there wouldn't be any English bars, so we never went.

Sorry for going on like that, but it's like I'm getting hit with revelation after revelation. My eyes are fully open for the first time … ever. So, back to today, feeling giddy I get in the car and even though it's still raining I'm going to have a drive out and see what I find.

I don't know if you've ever been to Cornwall but it's stunning. I'm amazed at how it has kept its original charm in a world full of concrete, steel and glass buildings and high-rise shards.

Tintagel is about 10 miles up the coast and believed to be the birth place of King Arthur. I'm not sure how much of that is true but the ruins are magical, and the view is breath taking. (Truthfully, I haven't *actually* got out and walked down the coastal path in the rain, but the information on Trip Advisor does say it's breath taking.)

I spend an hour or so just driving on the coastal road enjoying the beautiful views. I call into a little café in Boscastle and have a delicious cream tea, and I must say there is nothing nicer. Now, is it jam first, then cream, or cream first then jam? I know this is a bone of contention between Cornwall and Devon. I'll google it, so I don't look like an idiot (although googling that information alone does hold some idiocy). Anyway, according to The Telegraph it's jam then cream. Phew, heavens forbid I look foolish.

I run back to the car as it's pouring down and there right in the middle of where I need to look out, is a huge dollop of bird poo. I must have been from a Pterodactyl or an Ostrich, it's that big. Thankfully I have the screen wash, aka fairy liquid. As I reverse I squirt the window a good few times with my "screen wash" and the wipers start swishing. I turn around to check the rear as I reverse, and I see a bubble go past the window, and then another and another.

On this dismal day I can't imagine that any children playing out, let alone blowing bubbles. As I turn my head back to the front time seems to slow down. There are bubbles everywhere, blowing past all the windows. There, smeared amongst the bird poop, rain, fairy liquid and what actual remaining screen wash was in there, are bubbles, so many bubbles and suds all over the wind screen. I press for more screen wash to try to clean the poo away, but that just causes more and more bubbles. I have no idea what to do.

I look around and can now see people looking and pointing through the café window and they're all laughing. Now, the old me would have driven off in shame regardless of the way the car looked, just so I could get home quickly whilst dreading the lecture I would get from Andy. But, I just sit there and laugh. I stop squirting the liquid and just let the rain and the wipers clear away the mess and soap suds.

Laughing, I salute the café dwellers and set off again and look forward to giving the kids a good laugh at what a daft thing I did. Although it will probably be no surprise to them as my nickname for a while was "Sunspot", given when I thought I'd dripped some bleach on our brand-new carpet. I spend 20 minutes scrubbing it with all kind of stuff, but the white spot was still there, as bright as ever.

At this point I was on the verge of tears, dreading what Andy would say when he got home. I stood up, scratched my head and walked around the offending white spot and the bloody thing disappeared. What on earth? I moved back to where I was stood, and the spot appeared again. I moved a step to the right and it disappeared again. Turns out I had a tiny hole in one of the vertical blinds and the sun had shone through it.

So, it's safe to say that the kids know what I'm like.

I'm getting ready for Quiz Night, still smiling over my screen wash mishap. I put on my new black trousers and blush when I admire my bum in the mirror. These trousers are amazing! I've put on a simple white tailored shirt and wear a chunky necklace and bracelet. I hope I'm not overdressed but my jeans are in the wash, so I don't have any choice and a dress will be too much. Should I change? Maybe lose the jewellery? I take the necklace off and decide on some small earrings and just the bracelet.

The quiz is supposed to start at 8.00pm but I don't want to be late, so I set off 15 minutes early. I arrive at the pub at 7.51pm, I guess it's not that far after all. The pub seems quite busy as I can hear a lot of chatter coming through the doorway, and my first thought is to go back to the cottage. I don't walk into pubs alone. What was I thinking agreeing to come? What if they're not there? What if I they've changed their minds and I'm left on my own. God, I feel sick.

'Are you coming or going my love?' I'm asked by an elderly gentleman who has just arrived. Sod it!

'I'm coming.' I say, and he smiles and holds the door open for me, with a little bow.

Smiling, I thank him and look around for the team. The place is heaving, this must be a very popular quiz. I see someone waving frantically and it's Audrey, and I see that she's sat with Terry and John. I guess we're the team. I'm so thankful they're all there that I insist on buying the first round.

'I didn't expect to see so many people.' I say as I come over with a tray full of drinks.

'Oh yes, people all over the district come here for this.' Audrey enlightens me.

'So, does the team have a name?' I ask, curious as I've not been to a pub quiz before.

'We're called "Let's Have A Butcher's".' John looks proud as punch as he tells me their name. Before we can carry on our conversation, the DJ (are they called DJ's if they ask the questions at a pub quiz, or is it Quiz Master?) starts talking. Silence covers the pub like a school exam. The quiz is starting....

Question 1. What is the capital of Monaco? John says he knows that, it's where they do the grand prix – Monte Carlo. I know he's right so we all agree.

Question 2. Who played Dirty Den from East Enders?

'Ooh I know that one' says Audrey 'it's Lesley Grantham'. I have no idea, so I leave that to Audrey's soap expertise.

Question 3. Who wrote Sense and Sensibility? Everyone looks at each other blank. Now it's my turn.

'Jane Austen' I say.

'We'll go with that then' agrees John.

The questions go on and on. There are twenty in total, from 'the female to win the most Wimbledon's finals?' (I knew that one) to 'What is bigger, a blue whales tongue or his heart?' Terry gets that one.

We have so much fun. We laugh and drink, and I must admit to getting a little bit drunk. At the end of the quiz we're told to pass our answers to the left and then mark each other's papers, a bit like when we were at school and I love it! Why have I never done a pub quiz before?

The DJ plays some music to give us all time to replenish our beverages, and then he's ready to tell us the answers. Oddly, before John gives our papers over to "The Witty Warriors", he takes pictures of them on his phone, but before I can quiz Audrey on it the team to the right of us hands us their papers. They're called 'The Nutty Knitters' and they consist of five women, aged from around late twenties up to mid-seventies.

I would say in total there are about ten teams varying in sizes from couples through to the biggest team, seated to the left of us, which has seven men all aged around sixty.

It takes about ten minutes for the DJ/Quiz Master to tell us the answers, and then he instructs us to hand the papers back to the original teams.

To my surprise The Nutty Knitters cheer and high five each other even though they don't do quite so well and only manage 9 out of 20.

'Wow, that's their highest score!' says Audrey. 'Well done!' she tells them, and they raise their drinks in thanks.

"The Witty Warriors" pass our papers back. There's a funny look passing between John and the 'leader' of the warriors and if I'm not mistaken there's no love lost between the two. I lean over and ask Audrey what it's about.

'It's been going on a while now. We had our papers marked by The Warriors a couple of months ago. When we heard the results, we knew we'd won but one of the answers was 1965 and that's what we thought we'd put. Unfortunately, when we looked it said 1966. John was livid and accused The Warriors of sabotage and since then it's been like this.'

'Why do you let them mark the papers each time then?' Which seemed like an obvious solution but apparently John's pride wouldn't let him back down and he said that he wanted them to be the ones to mark the winning paper.

'Ahh, is that the reason he takes the pictures?'

'It is.'

Now I'm not normally competitive, but I can't stand cheats and now I'm willing for us to win, for Johns sake alone.

One thing that I pride myself on is my hand writing and they'd asked me to fill in the answers. As I have quite neat print there isn't usually any way it can be misread. Obviously, I may be mistaken but time will tell, either way we have proof now with Johns' pics.

We get our papers back and the Quiz Master (I found out that was his correct title) tells us all to raise our hands. He then tells us to lower our hands if our score is below

5/20. Most of us leave our hands up. Then they ask if anyone has a score above 10/20. 4 tables are left and, still smiling, The Nutty Knitters put their hands down.

Next, it's scores above 15/20 and there are only us and The Witty Warriors with our hands raised. We all look at each other but don't say anything. Our score is a whopping 19/20 but we don't know what the other team have.

The Quiz Master then asks scores above 16/20, both our team and The Warriors leave their hands up.

17/20, both team's hands stay up.

18/20, both team's hands stay up.

19/20 and we can't believe it, their hands go down. We've won!! You'd think that we'd won the lottery the amount of cheering going on. I was so pleased. We won fair and square. Unfortunately, John shouting 'In your face, in your face!' to the now not so Witty Warriors was a little unnecessary, but thankfully Terry stepped in before Kevin (The main warrior) threatened to knock the grin off John's face.

The night ended on a high, no harm done, and I was the team mascot until they remembered that I was going home on Saturday. I admit that sobering thought cast a dark cloud over me, but I could come back any time, so it wouldn't be a final farewell, it was more a 'see you later'. I took the opportunity to invite them all to the house on Friday night for a little thank you party and they were all thrilled. I even think I saw John blush.

I walked the short journey home with Audrey and Terry and bid them a cheery goodnight and for the first time in ages, when I got back to the cottage and closed the front door, I didn't cry, and I slept a deep, dreamless sleep.

Chapter 11

I woke the following morning feeling amazingly refreshed. It was a beautiful sunny day and I couldn't wait to go out. I had bought myself some paper, pencils, water colours and brushes when I was out the other day and had decided to go to the beach again and brush up on my painting. Pardon the pun! But this time I was going to Rock. It's a beautiful little town where the well-known St Enodoc's 12th century church sits, and as you can see the sea from there, it gives a beautiful back drop to the church and potentially my painting, at least in theory. I might be totally rubbish and nothing like Rolf Harris, so when I say "can you tell what it is yet? People would probably answer, "no".

It's been years since I've done any painting, but despite that I couldn't wait to start again, and was planning on doing a sunset. Unfortunately, I've just been so busy every night with my new friends. First world problems eh?

It's funny but this positive new me has got me thinking about Andy. Did it all go wrong because of me? Did I change so much? I must have let myself stop doing all this? There must have been a point where I just decided to give it up, but when? I remember painting pictures for the children's nursery's, in fact I still have them somewhere. I also did some for mum and dad, but I think that the older the children got, the busier I was with them, my degree, the business, the loss of my dad, the new house, work. Everything just muddles up into one big swirl of life and somewhere, in all of that, I lost myself.

I'm not saying that I'm putting all the blame on me and giving him a free pass. To be honest the way I feel now, I wouldn't want him back. 33 years. Not a few months but a lifetime. We went from children, to young adults to, ahem, middle aged, and in all that time he didn't feel he could say, 'Love, why don't you do something for you?' 'Why have you stopped painting?' 'Go out and enjoy yourself.'. He was happy for me to stop being the person I once was, whomever that was. Right now, right at this moment, I'm happy to be the person I am. At least for this week anyway.

So, moving forward today is about positivity and after my shower and a quick tidy round I make a packed lunch and get a couple of bottles of water (one for me and one for the painting) and set off to the beach.

It's a beautiful day. There are a few wispy cirrus clouds in the blue sky, and it's a bright sunny day. The sunlight shimmers on the Atlantic like Tiffany's diamonds. I can honestly say that I have never felt more relaxed or content anywhere. I take the short drive to Rock, smiling as I go, thankful the journey is 'sud-free'.

I park up and walk along the coastal path to the church. The walk is fresh with the sea air clearing my senses. The beach is dotted with dog walkers and then I'm at the church, which is half sunken in the ground. The fascinating history behind St Enodoc is that although the church dates from the 12th century, it was built in shifting sand dunes (Andy would have had a fit), which meant that for almost 300 years the church was almost totally buried in the sand and virtually unusable. But, to remain a church they had to hold one service a year, so the vicar and congregation had to climb in through a hole in the roof. I can just imagine my mum being told she had to climb into her church that way. She'd become an atheist in no time. Thankfully it's been renovated which means I can paint it, well the half that's visible anyway.

There are a couple of dog walkers around but other than that I have the place to myself, so I position myself on a stretch of grass showing the ocean behind the church.

I feel nervous at first. What if people see me painting and decide to have a look and it's dreadful, but they just nod politely and walk away shaking their heads, or worse still what if another artist comes and they *are* good and ... full on panic looming, but I give myself a mental shake.

What happened to the girl who would take her sketch book everywhere? Confident that the work was good. I would not and will not, ever be a Monet, but I was pretty good for an amateur and proud to hang my work in the house. I even donated a few to the local doctor's surgery and I believe they're still there, although that's not necessarily a good thing, it just means they haven't joined the 21st century and updated the surgery. Some of their magazines could be classed as collectors' items by now.

So, sufficiently shook, I begin.

The day has run away with me and I've painted a couple of pictures, had a walk around the inside of the church (without entering via the roof) and am now just driving up to the cottage. There's a familiar woman peering in through the window with a bag by her feet. I jump out of the car (it's not moving – I'd just pulled up) and run straight to my best friend, Chrissie.

'Oh my God, what are you doing here? I can't believe it!' I'm so happy to see her, my eyes glisten with joy.

'You've been away forever! It's not the same without you around.'

'Bloody hell it's only been a few days!' I laughed. You'd think I'd been abandoned on a desert island with only a football for company, when in fact I've only been away for a total of 5 days. Still, it's great that she's here and she can now see for herself why I love it so much.

Kettle on, biscuits out (I've not had any for a few days now so I'm proud that I still have some in) and we catch up in no time. I show her my Salsa moves and we have a good laugh at the quiz night dramatics. I thought she was going to pee when I told her about the suds! We laughed our heads off and it felt great to do so.

'It sounds like you've really settled in and you're coming home in a few days. What are you going to do?'

I don't have an answer.

'I know, you'll just have to keep popping back for long weekends or something, and I'll just have to come with you.' Chrissie is grinning at me, but she's hit a nerve and I feel a sinking in my stomach at the thought of going back home and everything that entails. 'What's wrong?' she asks.

'I don't know what I'm going to do is the honest answer. The people here have taken me under their wing, all courtesy of a chatterbox, but it's like I've always been here. Going back home just doesn't feel right, and I know that's just me avoiding reality and after all, this is just a holiday, but there just seems so much to do at home.'

I tell Chrissie all about the party I'm planning for tomorrow and about Karaoke tonight at the local pub. She stares at me in shock and then bursts out laughing. 'Fuck me. You? Singing? In public?'

'Yes, what's wrong with that?' I'm piqued by her bluntness and blushing at her language. We are like chalk and cheese. 'Cheeky sod. I'm sure I can get through one song without us being chucked out of Cornwall. Besides, with you by my side I'll be fine.'

She pretends to look unhappy but secretly I know that she'll love it. Chrissie has been known to appreciate having the limelight shone on her and tonight will be no exception, plus I'm not too worried as I only know a handful of people and I leave in a couple of days. The thought makes a lump appear in my throat and my eyes fill with tears. If I'm being honest with myself I think that it also has a lot to do with not wanting to face the reality of what awaits at home.

After a light evening meal, and a glass or two of Dutch courage (aka chardonnay) we get ourselves ready for the Karaoke fun that awaits us. It should be a good night and who knows, we might not be that bad after all. (Yes, and pigs might fly.)

The pub is surprisingly busy for 8.00pm on a Thursday. I think there are a few holiday makers in too, so it takes a while to spot the girls who invited me, Tina and Kay. They're waving manically in the corner, and I can see they've got a bottle of wine between them, so I gesture that we're going to the bar, buy another bottle and we weave our way over to them.

Hi ladies,' I give them both a hug and introduce my best friend. Pleasantries over with, I look around the crowded pub. 'I didn't think it would get so busy in here.' I say over the noise of someone murdering 'Sweet Caroline.' (Definitely, more sour than sweet.)

'Oh yes,' says Kay, 'it's always like this on karaoke night. It's a bit of a competition now to see who holds the golden cup for the week.'

'Oh, I love a good competition.' Chrissie rubs her hands together, eager to begin, just as I knew she would be.

'It's great!' Tina adds. 'Basically, at the end of the night, after everyone's sung a few songs, the DJ decides who's the best and hands the cup over. We've had it for the last two weeks running.' She grins at us. 'We sing Abba's Waterloo and it goes down a treat, but we usually get to sing more than one song anyway.'

I can see a glimmer in Chrissie's eye. She likes a bit of competition and will always try to win, no matter what it is. I will never, ever play Trivial Pursuit with her again. Christmas night 2012, board games with the family. Well, let's just say it was not her finest hour (she's one serious lady once the games begin.)

My mind drifts off to all the games I have at home. Who'll get them? Will we split the games 50/50? Will Andy want our 30-year-old tatty Monopoly, or Scrabble? It's so complicated, and what happens to our music? Do I need to start labelling stuff and working out who gets what? Oh God it's a mammoth task and I'm not sure I can …

'Hello, earth to Mandy, come in Mandy.' Chrissie and the girls are looking over at me, which isn't embarrassing, at all.

'Sorry, I was miles away.' I blush as I see Chrissie's face. 'I'm fine. Honest.' I'm no good at telling lies and I'm not fooling anyone, but now is not the time to start thinking about these things, so it's shoulders back again and focus on what's important right now, and that's my new friends (and my old one).

There's a couple of folders being handed around with all the song choices in it and you just put your name and song choice on a piece of paper and give it to the DJ. Luckily you can have more than one song which is great as I have my eye on a few. I think the wine has loosened my tongue and hardened my nerve, and I've only had half a glass! Oh, plus the two at home, I remind myself.

'Alright my lovelies!' Shouts a male voice from behind me. It's John, who apparently loves Karaoke and Elvis is his favourite. What a dark horse he's turned out to be. Next, in come Audrey and Terry. They love

101

singing anything by Dolly Parton and Kenny Rogers – now I know why there was an instant connection with them, I smile and look at Chrissie, and laughing she rolls her eyes and calls me a 'Saddo'.

The drinks flow and our song requests are entered. Tina and Kay are the first to get up from our group, and they sing 'Dancing Queen', another Abba favourite of theirs. They even do a little dance with it, and don't look at the words on the screen at all. I can see why they've won the cup for the last two weeks. We all cheer and clap when they've finished.

Next up is our very own Elvis aka John the butcher, who sings 'In the ghetto'. I always cry at this song and tonight is no exception.

'John you were amazing, and I can honestly say you're the best Cornish Elvis I've ever heard.' I hug him and as usual he blushes, but mumbles 'thanks' in reply.

Drinks and laughter flow through the night. Audrey and Terry do a Dolly and Kenny duet of 'Islands in the Stream' and they're not bad either (I wouldn't tell them, but Terry is better than Audrey, but despite that they manage between them). Then it's Chrissie's turn. I've picked Gloria Gaynor – I will survive, and Chrissie has gone with Bonnie Tyler's – Total Eclipse of the Heart. She's up first and I drink more wine.

Chrissie starts singing. She's not picked an easy song but other than a few off notes she's not bad at all and judging by the applause, everyone else enjoyed it too.

Oh God, now it's my turn. I walk up to the stage like I'm walking the gang plank and Jack Sparrow has a sword in my back.

I think the words are quite appropriate, but it would be better if I could see them properly. OK, this is easy, I can do it, everyone's watching, I can't do it, don't be silly you'll be fine. Yes, I will be fine. I CAN do it! The music starts, and my heart beat is thumping along to the bass.

'At first, I was afraid, I was petrified ...' You can say that again! My singing is a little quiet, I even ask if the mikes on and he says it is and I just need to sing louder. 'KEPT THINKING I COULD ...' There seems to be technical difficulties as the microphone screeches at top note. 'Stay away from the speakers.' The DJ tells me, raising his eyes to heaven. Cheeky sod.

I can see my friends laughing their heads off at my poor beginning but they're still cheering and giving me the thumbs up. Their encouragement gives me the push I need, so I give myself one of my mental shakes and start to sing properly. Hey, I don't sound too bad, but given that my start couldn't have been worse, and the only reason Simon Cowell would be banging at my door is to tell me to shut up, I soldier on and end up enjoying every minute – can't say that for the audience though.

When I finish, my friends are cheering so much you'd think they were at a Take That concert and Robbie had just turned up and surprised everyone. Needless to say, we have a fantastic night. Chrissie and I sing Sonny and Cher's 'I got you babe', and Chrissie finishes off with Nena's '99 Red Balloons'. I think the previous songs must have got her into the swing of this, as she sings this one perfect. I honestly didn't realise she was so good. To be honest, I don't think she did either. The night ends on an absolute high as Chrissie has won this week's Gold Cup. Even Tina and Kay, who seemed a little competitive at first, praise her on the win and Chrissie gives the cup to Tina, so they can return it the following week.

The night is over too soon and we all say goodnight and head off to our respective homes. It's a lovely balmy night and we may both be a little tiddly. One thing I'm noticing tonight, which I didn't before is how narrow the roads are. For some reason I keep walking into the houses on either side of the road.

'D'ye know wot luv?' Chrissie slurs at me and her Manchester accent comes out so much stronger when she's drunk. 'a think am a bi' pished!'

'No way! I think I am too.' I say to the Chrissie in the middle. 'Did you have a good night then?'

'Did I ever! Your new mates are a fuckin' blast. No wonder ya dint wanna come 'ome. Buram glad y'ar, coz ave missed ya, an a fuckin' luv ya. Ur me bezzie mate!'

'You're my bezzie mate too and I love you to bits, but I am really sad to be going home.'

We arrive back at mine and for some reason I'm having trouble opening the door. Well actually, I'm having trouble putting the key in the lock as the bloody thing keeps moving, or is it me that's moving? I can't tell but by some fluke I manage to do it and we stagger in.

'Am fucked Mand and am go-in-a bed. Nigh' luv.' And off she totters or staggers. I follow suit and sit on the bed, quietly laughing to myself about the nights events.

'Wha' ya bleedin' laughin' at ya daft cow?' Chrissie shouts through the wall. Maybe I wasn't so quiet after all.

I wake the following morning, fully clothed on top of the bed, with a rather furry mouth and a very poorly head. The sun is streaming in through the thin curtains and the birds are singing. Usually, this is what I love about being here, but today it's like torture and every high-pitched note each bird sings are like tiny hammers in my head. I didn't think I'd drank quite so much but I guess I did. Oh God, I remember singing now, so yes, I must have drunk a lot.

'Arrghh' I hear Chrissie groan from the next room. At least we both feel rough together.

'I'm going to put the kettle on,' I say as I stumble past her door. I head for the bathroom first. I pee first then go to wash my hands and I see my reflection in the mirror. Bloody hell, I really do look like Ken Dodd this morning, and only after he's been to a Kiss concert with last night's eye makeup smudged down my cheeks. I throw a bit of water on my face but that doesn't really help so I give up and brush my teeth - at least that takes the furry feeling away.

'Oh luv, I feel as bad as you look.' Chrissie laughs when she sees me.

'Ditto.' I groan.

We spend the morning lounging, showering and lounging again. Knowing I must get some food and drink in for tonight's party I drag myself and then Chrissie up off the sofa and we head off to the shops to buy supplies and some wine – although the wine makes us both visibly blanch and I'm sure our skin has dropped a shade or two paler - but as northern women we refuse to be beaten. We drop the supplies back at the cottage and go for a walk on the beach to clear away the cobwebs.

'What's up luv?' Chrissie asks as I must have been miles away.

'I'm just thinking how nice this is and how sad I am to leave.' I sigh and stop to look out to sea. 'I've never met a more welcoming, friendly bunch of people in my whole life. They have taken me in without even knowing me. Although they did know a lot more about me than I would have liked in the beginning, and obviously you can't have any secrets in a village with such impressive jungle drums. But, none of them judged, they all just accepted me. I feel sad, that's all.'

Chrissie leans over, puts her arm around me and says in her special loving way. 'No one likes a cry baby.'

We get back to the cottage and sort out the food. I've got some tortilla chips and dips, some crudités as well and an assortment of sushi, sandwiches and salad. All set. The wine is chilling in the fridge, the citronella candles are burning around the garden – which looks lovely as Audrey has hung jam jars all around the small garden. The tea light candles look gorgeous inside them and there's a larger one burning on the table.

Everything is set, I'm wearing my jeans and my new floaty top which seems to fit better than it did on our shopping trip - and cost so much that I had a phone call from the bank to check I wasn't a victim of credit card fraud! My hair is wavy and hanging around my shoulders and looks a very healthy auburn.

'You look amazing love!' Chrissie said when she saw me. 'You seem to have changed and I'm not quite sure what it is, but this place must have special powers as it's worked its magic on you.' I feel proud at the compliment, but let's be honest here, it's not that long ago that I was sat in a foul smelling dressing gown, looking like I lived in a sleeping bag outside Topshop in town, surrounded by crumbs, wrappers and god knows what else! However, that aside, I feel good. A little sad, but good all the same.

By 8.30pm everyone has arrived and as I expected they all brought something. John had cooked some chipolatas, Mary has brought a gorgeous looking toffee cheesecake (which apparently is talked about all over the county according to Audrey), Tina cooked some wonderful garlic and herb buttered king prawns, Kay has brought some fresh strawberries and cream and Audrey and Terry, some wine.

By the end of the night, we're all a bit sloshed – again – and the food has gone down a storm. In fact, there's hardly anything left. I was ordered to put some into a couple of Tupperware dishes for our journey home before anyone could tuck in, not that we were complaining. It looks like Chrissie and I have a great lunch for tomorrow.

At around 11.00 everyone went their respective ways, Audrey and Terry went first as they would see us both off in the morning. Kay, Tina, Mary and John all left together and I'm sure there was a glint of moisture in John's eyes. They all said how sad they were that I was going and to come back as often as I could. We exchanged email addresses and phone numbers and promised to stay in touch and I knew they meant it. To be honest, it was quite emotional. I had only been here a week, yet I felt like I was leaving family. I was going back to real life and I wasn't looking forward to that at all.

This beautiful little cottage and the lovely new friends I made had given me respite from all the sadness, bitterness and uncertainty that was to come, and for that I was extremely grateful.

I've just realised what the niggling feeling I've been having is, I think it's called optimism.

PART TWO

THE MIDDLE

Chapter 12

It had been a few weeks since we had returned from Cornwall and our stop off to see my daughter. Thankfully she was more than happy to put Chrissie up too and we enjoyed a couple of days with Molly and the family. The twins were adorable, and it hurt so much to have to say goodbye to them all and head back up to Cheshire, but there hadn't been a spare minute since our return.

In the pile of mail behind my front door, there was one from my solicitor saying that he needed to see me, and could I book an appointment as soon as possible. Unfortunately, I was so busy with work that I still hadn't gotten around to it.

What I had managed to do however, was to clear out all of Andy's clothes; granted with the help of Chrissie, several roles of bin liners and a couple of bottles of

Chardonnay. It was so hard packing them up, as each item of clothing held a memory and some still had his smell and hints of his favourite aftershave Tom Fords, Neroli Portofino. I was just about to spray some on me when, Chrissie leapt at me ninja style, and grabbed the bottle off me saying, 'Not on my watch sister.'

I messaged Andy and told him that his clothes were in the garage and to collect them before I gave them all to the local charity shop. I had hoped, despite what he had done, we would remain amicable but sadly it seemed it was destined to be an acrimonious divorce.

I know that it was petty, especially given what I had just said, but in all honesty, it wasn't just that I was trying to gain a little control, the truth was it hurt to see all his clothes there just waiting for him to open the wardrobe and get dressed. The house felt huge when it was just Andy and me living there, but with just me in there, it was enormous. Worse still, I knew it had lost its heart.

I was leaning more and more towards selling it, which upset me more than I expected, especially given that it was all Andy's style inside it and not mine. Still, I couldn't help looking around with an aching heart, each room flooded with memories of the children and our marriage. But, whenever I was feeling like this I remembered Billy's words, *'wherever you are mum, is home',* and it made me feel a whole lot better.

I had been speaking to the children regularly and keeping them updated with all events and I was in touch, as promised, with the Cornwall crew. Billy had told me that his dad was still going ahead with his move to Australia with 'Bloody Zooey' and that I should now start to think about myself and be positive and move forward. The house wasn't home anymore, and as far as he was concerned I should do what was right for me and not anyone else. (For the baby of the family he's got a very level head).

Following that conversation and as a first step, well second if you count sticking all Andy's clothes in the garage, I had decided that I had to stop calling Andy's new girlfriend 'The Young Bloody Australian Physiotherapist called Zooey' as not only was it a mouthful it was a little childish, so I had now reduced it to the more mature 'Bloody Zooey'. Soon I'd be calling her BZ - That was progress, wasn't it?

The following week I received another letter from my solicitor asking me to make an appointment as soon as possible. Apparently, he had important matters to discuss and although I didn't want to know what they were, I also I knew that I couldn't keep procrastinating. I rang Chrissie and asked her to come with me and I made the appointment, feeling sick the whole time. They did ask if I could bring any documents from the business that might show my involvement.

I searched the whole house for any paperwork, anything from the business and I found nothing. Andy must have been in at some point and taken everything, but when? It had to have been when I was in Cornwall or at work. I decided at that point to get the locks changed. Was that a bad idea? Was I overreacting? I didn't know anymore. All I did know was that the safe was empty as were all the drawers in his home office. But it was more than that. I know it's still his home, but to think that he could have been here, walking around like he owned the place (which technically he did but I'm not feeling very rational right now). Did he bring Zooey? Has she been in my home? Would they have had sex in the house? On my bed? In the lounge? I got myself a little worked up just thinking about it and only just managed to calm myself with a bit of meditation before an anxiety attack came on.

The weeks following the first solicitor appointment where my mind was blank, and I was still in shock, I had a light bulb moment when I remembered that the business was set up using the money my dad left me in his will, and I was down as company secretary (which now only meant that occasionally I had to sign some documents, where in the beginning it meant that I had to do all the accounts, admin and marketing etc). Unfortunately, I wasn't sure how to get confirmation. Lucky for me, Chrissie and I have watched enough crime dramas to know that any important paperwork was usually kept in the culprit's home office or work office. And there was a lot of information in Andy's work office. And I still had a key. The only thing I had to work out now was when to go and at what time as his office was in a shared block and they had 24-hour security guards.

I gave myself a fortnight for the solicitor's appointment, so I had to get a hustle on and work out a plan and carry it out and given the speed in which Bloody Zooey (I wasn't quite ready to start naming her after a rapper just yet) had put her feet, quite comfortably, under the table I reckoned that Andy would have told security that I wasn't to be allowed entry.

Luckily, I had Chrissie on my side. One of the security guards (Daniel) was infatuated with her, and I knew that he worked weekday nights, so I had quite a few opportunities to put my plan into action. Although, I still hadn't quite worked out a plan.

First things first, I just needed to confirm that Daniel would be there, and Andy would not. This meant that I had to ring up the main desk to check. I had to be clever though as Andy could never know I had telephoned, so I disguised my voice by putting a hanky over the mouthpiece like the baddies always do on television. (Clever, even if I do say so myself).

'Hello.' I muffled. 'Can I speak to Kevin please?'

'Hi Mrs Harper!' said Kevin. 'It's me, are you ill? Your voice sounds croaky.' Bloody hell, I guess that didn't work. Ironically Kevin wasn't normally the sharpest knife in the drawer but obviously this was one of his better days. However, he did say that Andy wouldn't be in for the next 10 days as he was on holiday, in Spain (probably sat in an English pub watching football). I thanked him and said yes, I had a cold and hung up.

'10 days?' said Chrissie after she'd stopped laughing. I had thought masking my voice with the old 'hankie over the receiver' trick was rather a clever idea, but her response had been less complementary.

'For fuck sake! A hanky?' she said, in between gasping for air and laughing hysterically. I tell you, some people need to appreciate my new-found espionage skills and be more complimentary with my attempts.

We sat down, wine to hand not necessarily being our best idea, and came up with an amazing fool proof plan.

Well, it was a good plan.

Actually, it was probably a terrible plan, but it was the only one we could come up with on 2 bottles of wine.

The idea was that Chrissie would turn up when Daniel was on his shift. She would wear something a little revealing but not too slutty and obvious and she would make some drama up about her car breaking down around the corner. Daniel would obviously step up as the knight in shining armour and offer to help. I would slip in, go to the office, get the paperwork (although I had no idea where it would be) and slip quietly back down the stairs. Then when I was on the ground floor I would ring Chrissie, so she knew to somehow distract Daniel again, and I would slip out, unseen.

See, fool proof. What could go wrong?

Chapter 13

With just 4 days left until (and please say this in a deep, dramatic voice) 'Operation Magpie' was a go, I was panicking. Was this a criminal offence? Did it serve a minimum sentence of 10-15 in a maximum-security prison? Should I stop watching CSI?

The questions were flooding through my mind day and night, and I was having a hard time focusing at work which as a bereavement counsellor it is imperative that I at least remember who, or what, the client has lost. For example, I was with Mrs Chadwick today who I thought had lost her husband (innocent mistake, I'd muddled her up with Mrs Chesworth). My mind wandered, and I refocused when she started talking about missing having him on the bed, and my innocent reply was …

'You must miss the physical side of your relationship. Intimacy does play a big part.' In which she looked at me funny, stood up and said …

'I don't know what you get up to with your dog but let me assure you there was no 'intimacy' had at all! Then she walked out. (No harm done there then.)

I sat in the room for a while until my supervisor came and asked me to go to her office. Oh god, this was worse than being called into the headmaster's office at school. Legs shaking, heart pounding I went to see her.

'Amanda,' she said with a menacing tone. 'let me ask you something first.' Well, here it comes, sit tall, back straight and take whatever punishment she meters out. 'Do you have sugar in your tea? I should know by now but my memory's rubbish when it comes to those things.' What the …?

'Oh, erm no sugar thanks.'

Janet made me a cup of tea, opened the biscuits and asked me if I was OK. Rookie mistake.

'No, no I'm really not OK.' I moan. 'My husband has left me for a woman half my age, well not really half but she might as well be as she looks it, and she's Australian and a physiotherapist, and all the while I'm rattling around in a mausoleum of a house and he's taken the paperwork that proves it was my money that set up his business and I need it to show my solicitor who I find attractive but my body is going south and no one is going to want to see that and I miss my new friends in Cornwall and want to take up Salsa classes here but no one will come with me and I'm not sure I could do it on my own anyway and what if

I meet a new man and have to start shaving my legs all the time? Well, erm … that's it for now.'

I stare at her with what I think can only be described as a manic expression on my face (and panting heavily because it's not that easy to say all that at once) as she says, 'And how does that make you feel?' But then winks and I take a deep breath and then start laughing and then to my horror, crying.

'I don't know what's gotten into me.' I snivel as she passes me the ever-present box of tissues in a counsellor's office (that's one good thing, we never ever run out of tissues). I take the proffered cup of tea and biscuit and dunk it before saying, 'I feel like I'm falling apart. Everything I've known since being 14 has gone in a heartbeat, and I know he's not died, but somehow this feels worse. There's no closure, for want of a better word. He's out there, living the dream, having sex all the time with his 'Young…' sorry, with 'Bloody Zooey' and I'm left picking up all the pieces. How am I going to separate all the things in the house? Who's is what? We bought everything together. We didn't meet when we were adults and conjoin two homes into one. We started together, the two of us who then became the five of us. I've not even seen him since he left, and I'm not even sure I want to, but for him not to even try to talk to me, means that I don't even get the pleasure of screaming at him or even hanging up the phone on him.' I take a sip of my tea and try to ignore the biscuit floating in it. (Tip – Never dunk when talking.)

Janet is so lovely and mumsy. She's about 5ft 1", round in a cute cuddly way and I guess her age to be mid

60's. She has grey/white hair, cut in a layered bob which makes her blue eyes stand out and she is always smiling. She has a few grandchildren and I know she bakes with them every weekend. Basically, she's the best kind of grandma.

Janet takes her glasses off and rubs the bridge of her nose. Taking a deep breath, she says, 'The bastard has left you right in the shit, hasn't he?'

'Erm …' I have no words, and my mouth drops open. (Not my best look.)

'What? Didn't you think I could swear?' She laughs.

In the end, we agree that it's probably best if I leave early and cancel my appointments for the next few days while I get my head together. I speak to Chrissie and tell her what's happened, but I don't get the reply I was expecting.

'You need a new you!' she announces. (Do I?) 'I'm going to book you to get a haircut, nails and make over tomorrow. That will help. Trust me, I've been there.'

I agree, as I have nothing left to lose.

It's three days to go until (deep dramatic voice) 'Operation Magpie' and I'm at Chrissie's hairdressers. I'm having my hair cut and styled into a wavy concave bob with a long fringe and centre parting. Jonathan, the hairdresser, who is camp as Christmas is telling me that I need a hot oil treatment daahling and when was the last time I had my hair cut daahling and do I know how many split ends I have?

'Look at them daahling, Look!' And he thrusts my terrible split end hair in front of my eyes. Personally, I thought my hair was quite healthy but 'in for a penny' as they say. I ignore what's going on and read my book. I know there's hot oil, a colour, a cut, drying, curling, tutting, more cutting a little more curling but I feel so muddled that I force myself to relax and get stuck into reading and the regular supply of tea (and those gorgeous little biscuits in the red wrappers) when suddenly, he says, 'Ta dah!'

I look up and there's a younger woman looking back at me. My hair looks amazing! I look amazing. I have no fancy clothes or makeup on, I'm still wearing the unflattering shapeless black cape/gown and it's fastened under my chin (well one of them), but I still look great. I can't speak (which seems to be a recurring thing).

'Oh God.' He says, 'You don't like it?' He's bordering on panic mode now, which helps me find my voice. I just look at him and say,

'Like it? No. I love it!' My lovely new hair, which is now 3 inches shorter bounces in agreement around my face as the shiny chestnut brown gives way to golden ends. The perfect Ombre or is it Balyage? I don't now and don't care. All I know is that I love my new hairstyle. Slowly but surely, I feel Mandy coming back. I didn't realise I'd lost her until she'd started creeping to the surface.

While I'm doing a very good impression of narcissism, Jonathan tells me to go and see Julie who will do my nails and then Stella who will do my makeup.

By the time I'm finished I've been in there for 5 hours. I ordered sandwiches for everyone at one point and had an absolute scream listening to their horror stories of waxing, acrylic nails, sunbeds and even spray tanning a transvestite gentleman who insisted on wearing his own black lacy Brazilian knickers.

'I'm telling you' says Julie, 'those knickers don't cover that much on us women and our lady gardens are flat, but all I can say is that he went home that day with one white testicle and one brown one!' We all fall about laughing and it feels a bit heady, as though a weight has been lifted from my shoulders.

I leave there after paying a small fortune, worth every penny, looking stunning and feeling it, and meet Chrissie at the local Italian for an early dinner. I can see her looking gorgeous as usual, but she just looks right past me as I'm walking up to her.

'Heyy! Have you gone blind?' I say as I approach. She does a double take and then just stares at me.

'Oh. My. God. You look fuckin' amazin'!' She makes me do a twirl and then gets her phone out to take pictures. Laughing I drag her into the restaurant. I feel like the hair, make up, clothes, nails and I'm proud to say a little weight loss, have made me feel wonderful and after we order a bottle of wine she shows me the photos. I can't believe that the woman staring back is me. I haven't really taken much time looking at myself lately but now I can see the weight loss as well as everything else. I feel like a new woman. (This new lady is staying.)

After we order I make a quick telephone call to the salon and arrange to go and see Stella in the morning for a lesson on applying make-up and a list of what products to buy.

'I can't get over the change in you Mand. You were always gorgeous, not that you would have believed me, but now … now you're a fuckin' stunner! I just hope that useless, soon-to-be-ex-husband of yours gets to see what he's been missing!'

I look around to see if anyone can hear her expressive praise, but there aren't many people in and they're all wrapped up in their own conversations. Even though I feel like a million dollars, all I can think is that we have just a few days left until I turn into a criminal and I'm dreading it.

I tell Chrissie my fears and she just jiggles her boobs at me while saying, 'Are you implying that these babies won't be enough of a distraction? I'm insulted.' She feigns outrage and we both laugh. We have agreed to meet up after work on Thursday for 'Operation what the hell am I doing?' I change the name back and forth between this and 'Operation Magpie', as the closer I get the more terrified I become. To change the subject, I ask her if she's got any gossip. She says no but looks a little sheepish, which is a surprise as I've never known her to look like that.

'Chri-ssieee!' I let the last two vowels drag out as I slowly say her name (like when you're making your kids tell the truth). 'What's going on?'

Just as she's about to speak the waiter arrives with our pizza to share and she talks effusively about our dinner, I guess in the hope she'll distract me and forget. 'Well?' I refuse to let her back away from this and give her my best 'mum look'. It seems to do the trick.

'OK. Do you remember the guy I met at the christening who was an arse regarding the woman who'd been married 5 times?' I nod and 'humph' (Miss Piggy style) to show my disgust and solidarity. 'Well as you know he's been texting me, but there's been one every day and I've ignored them for weeks. I mean, I just thought he was a dick-cum-stalker but in the end, instead of deleting them without reading them, I read one.' For the first time ever, she blushes. In all the years I've known Chrissie I have never, ever seen her blush. She swears like a sailor, is about as diplomatic as Prince Philip and is usually the one making *me* blush, but here she is, looking sheepish AND blushing. What the hell did he put in those texts?

It turns out that it was nothing mnemonic of 50 shades, mores the pity, he just kept apologising. He was bitterly ashamed for judging her and had never wanted to remove his foot from his mouth faster. She was the first woman to pique his interest in a long time and he was mortified that he'd offended her and wanted to make it right.

'So, do you believe him?' I asked.

'I think so. I mean yes, I do. He could have just left it and never thought about me again and it's been weeks since the Christening. But what do *you* think?' She looks at me with eager eyes.

Now, just pause for a minute. Bearing in mind that I've known Chrissie for 15, 20, erm well, clearly a lot of years, and ahem a few husbands, she has never asked me what I think about any guy and especially not with 'eager eyes'. I look back at her with a different view. This woman, this strong amazing woman, this strong amazing independent woman (bloody hell get on with it) is just like the rest of us and I believe her heart grew 3 sizes that day (my kids loved The Grinch).

'I think that he deeply regrets what he's done and that second chances are there for a reason. So, give him a second chance.' She grins back at me like a teenager who's just been told that not only can she go to the party on Friday night but, she doesn't have to be in until midnight.

'I was hoping you were going to say that. I'll ring him later. I can't do with all this text messaging and I'll know if he's serious by his voice.' She breathes out deeply, as though she's been holding her breath waiting for my answer.

'Now, what the fuck are you worrying about?' And Chrissie is back in the room.

Chapter 14

It's D-Day. The countdown has ended and today is the day I become a petty thief. I go through my wardrobe and pull out my black jeans (yes, I now own some of these too), black polo neck, black hoody and black baseball cap (hoody and cap recent purchase due to oncoming criminal activity) and my black boots. I'm hoping no one will recognise me and I'll blend in with the night. I've even bought some black camouflage paint, not sure why but it seemed the right thing to do at the time. I'm just about to get dressed when I hear the door and Chrissie letting herself in.

'Hi, Butch Cassidy's here, is the Sundance Kid ready?' She shouts.

'Sshhh,' I shush, as though I live in a shared commune and everyone will recognise the relevance, 'I'll be down in a minute. Put the kettle on, I need a brew and a biscuit to calm my nerves.' I can hear Chrissie laughing but it doesn't help to sway the fear in the pit of my stomach. In a few hours I will be a criminal.

Chrissie turns as I walk in the kitchen.

'Aha ha ha ha ha!' She is hysterical with laughter. Clearly, she's finding something funny, but I have no idea what she's laughing about and say so, which only makes her laugh more, until tears are rolling down her face and she's holding onto the worktop as she bends over to get rid of the ache in her stomach.

I look at my reflection in the hall mirror. OK, so maybe I didn't need the camouflage paint on my cheeks, but she doesn't have to be so rude about it.

After cleaning my face, I remain in the black ensemble, we sit and have our cups of tea.

'What were you thinking?' Chrissie asks me, still laughing but quieter now.

'I didn't want to be recognised.' Although I'm adamant that I have made the right choice of criminal attire, I feel the need to justify my look.

'Recognised? Don't you think that a 47-year-old woman wearing, what is pretty much a teenage gang outfit, will stand out?' Well, I guess when she puts it like that. 'And as for the Rambo look? Oh God,' she starts laughing again. 'You looked hilarious.' I start to see the funny side and agree I might have gone a step too far. She tells me to change my clothes, but I refuse. Gang clothes aren't cheap and when will I ever get to wear them again? And, just a thought, where do these kids get the money to buy them?

Without the Rambo stripes I look reasonable and I promise only to put the cap on if I feel it 'absolutely necessary' (which for me means the minute she's gone off to distract Daniel). One thing I didn't think of is that they will have CCTV. What if I'm seen? What if they've changed the alarm codes on the safe? What if the guard phones the police? What if I stop thinking and just get on with it?

I voice all my concerns to Chrissie, who I'm pleased to say has now stopped laughing, and she just tells me calmly again, about the plan.

The Plan

1. Chrissie is going to walk into the building and ask the security guard directions, whilst flirting with him outrageously and wearing a dress so low cut you can almost see her Brazilian. (I recently found out what one was, and let me tell you, they are *not* pleasant.)

2. He will be so distracted that he won't see me slip in through the door and go up the back stairs to the first-floor office.

3. As I still have a key, I will let myself into said office and search the filing cabinets and safe for obvious secure places for hiding important documents.

4. Once the paperwork is recovered I will lock up the office and use the back stairs to return to the ground floor where I'll ring Chrissie.

5. She'll have an imaginary argument with the caller i.e. boyfriend who is letting her down at short notice and therefore distract security guard fully.
6. I will sneak out and she will pretend she's so upset she'll have to go home and take his phone number, which he'll obviously give.

Sounds simple enough … Doesn't it?

Now don't get me wrong. This is not Trump Tower we're trying to get into, it's just a 5-storey office block that belongs to Harper Business Ltd. Their office is on the first floor and they rent the rest of the office space out.

We decide to go at night, well about 8.30pm so that way Chrissie's story sounds realistic. We arrive at 8.25pm. I'm sweating profusely, hyperventilating a little and possibly even suffering a little tachycardia.

'No wonder you're sweating under all that clobber.' She shakes her head.

'This isn't going to work.' I cry.

'Come on Daniel Craig, it's going to be fine.'

'I don't want to end up somebody's bitch and I really don't suit orange overalls.

'Bloody hell, I'm cancelling your Netflix subscription as soon as this is done.' Shaking her head at me she adds more red lipstick, fluffs her hair, pulls her boobs up inside her dress (held securely in place courtesy of some heavy-duty fashion tape thus enhancing the already enhanced cleavage), takes one last look at herself and says, 'Right, let's do this.' And before I can say 'Orange is the New Black', she's off and walking towards the building.

I take a deep breath, wipe my sweaty palms on my jeans, put my cap on (she won't know) and run to the side of the building, stopping just next to the entrance door. Chrissie knocks on the door and waves at Daniel.

'He's coming,' she whispers. I feel sick.

'Hello,' I hear Daniel say. 'How can I help you?'

'It's Daniel, isn't it?' Chrissie uses her sexy voice.

'Erm, yes miss erm I mean ma'am.' I giggle in my head as I know she's not going to let the 'ma'am' bit go.

'Can I come in Daniel? I'm a bit lost and I thought you might remember me and help. I'm Amanda's friend.'

Daniel mumbles something I can't quite hear but he's obviously invited her in and I can hear her saying, 'Oh you do remember, and do I really look like a ma'am to you?'

I can tell by his silence and her quiet laughter that he's mesmerised and possibly wondering whether she's got her dress on back to front as he's sure he shouldn't be able to see her belly button.

I take this as my cue to pop in 'undetected'. Chrissie is chatting away to Daniel and showing him Google maps on her phone and I sneak in and head towards the back stairs. Undetected so far, my stealth like moves are obviously second to none.

I open the door to the first floor, thankfully it's all clear. I slowly head towards Andy's office, checking the other rooms as I go. I'm just about to unlock his door when I'm spotted. All the hard work for nothing, all the planning and gangster clothes for what? There's someone looking right back at me from inside Andy's office. I think it's a teenage boy, but why would Andy have a teenage boy locked inside his office? And I must admit he does look a little thuggish. In my panic, I raise both arms as I've been caught out. And oddly, so does he. I put my hands down, and so does he. I then realise what an idiot I am, as it's just my own reflection in the window. Well, at least if nothing else, this outfit knocks years off me.

I carry on and am in Andy's office with ease. The locks haven't been changed, so I go to the safe and thankfully the code hasn't either. He obviously doesn't think I have it in me to be a little sneaky, well more fool you Andrew Harper! The safe has lots of papers inside and some money, but none of the required documents. I close it and make sure it's locked. Don't want any burglars coming in, I laugh to myself.

Where to look now? I go through the filing cabinets which I have all the keys for, but other than staff contracts and building contracts from all the past, present and future builds there is nothing to show I have any financial status in the business.

Not to be put off I check his desk. The bottom drawers are not locked and therefore naturally don't hold any important papers. The top drawer is locked, as I knew it would be, but I don't have a key for that and as I've looked everywhere else the documents must all be in there. I'm sure I can jimmy the lock with something. Maybe I have some hair grips in my bag, I think I just need to jiggle a couple in the lock and it should open. Unfortunately, I have no bag or hair grips, nor the ability to pick a lock.

I sit forward and drop my head into hands. This is hopeless. What am I doing? Tears fill my eyes. One, because this will probably be the last time I'll see the place and two, because I'm no spy. Daniel Craig can relax, I won't be needed to fill in for the next 007.

I wipe my eyes on my hoodie and I see that I've messed the papers on his desk. I straighten them up, as obviously I don't want him to know I've been here, and guess my utter surprise and overwhelming gratitude, when there on his desk - not filed away safely, not even in a drawer but carefully set out in neat little folders is the Christmas present of all Christmas presents - the bank transfer from my inheritance, the documents from Companies House showing when the business became a Limited Company and the cherry on top, it shows me listed as a company secretary. The Post-It note on top says, 'Here are the documents you requested.' God bless Margaret, his uber efficient secretary.

I gather all the paperwork together, lock everything up and head back downstairs. I ring Chrissie as planned and she plays up the argument on the phone. This is my cue to leave undetected.

'Oh, Mrs Harper?'

Shit!

'Hi Daniel!' I squeak.

'I didn't see you come in ma'am.' He looks at the door and then at the entrance to the stairs.

'I saw you talking to this lady, so I just popped up to the office to get some things I needed.' I'm talking a hundred miles an hour and several octaves higher and can't seem to stop. 'Chrissie? Is that you? Wow, what are you doing here?'

Chrissie ends the call with her imaginary lover and plays up seeing me.

'Mandy?' she's got her back to Daniel and is giving me the look that says, "do not mess this up".

'She was lost' said Daniel, helping.

'I was lost' said Chrissie, 'and I thought I'd ask someone I know for directions, as I've seen Daniel before and you can't always trust strangers, can you? But, now you're here you can help me.' She links her arms through mine and before I know it we're saying a cheery goodbye to a rather flustered and red-faced Daniel and walking out with me telling Chrissie she can follow my car and I'll direct her to wherever she needs to go. With our backs straight and standing tall, we walk out of the building and around the corner where we fall about laughing until we're hiccupping and crying.

It turns out that my 'soon-to-be-ex' was thankfully not into espionage, or he hasn't watched as many crime drama's as me and hasn't told the night staff to stop me going into the building. All the planning was for nothing, the outfits (mine and Chrissie's), the flirting, the panicking – all for naught.

Poor Daniel, one minute he has a 'cougar' flirting with him and next he has Puff Mummy in da house ruining it for him. All that preparation. All that worry. All that beautifully presented paperwork. There's a saying, 'when life throws you lemons you make lemonade'. Well, this time the lemon is going into several gin and tonics. I think we deserve them, naturally along with our BAFTA's and employment contracts with MI5.

We call at Chrissie's first, so she can change out of her 'belly button viewing' dress and into something a little more comfortable and so she can also lend me a top to wear, so my outfit can never be seen in public again.

After all that adrenaline we're both famished and agree that dinner in our regular Italian restaurant is just what we need. Giovanni finds us a table in a quiet corner, and we peruse our wares and drink a couple of large G&T's whilst waiting for our dinner.

'Well' says Chrissie after taking a long drink of her favourite tipple.

'Well indeed!' I reply shaking my head in wonderment. 'This is definitely a story that will give my children a laugh and will no doubt be told for years to come. Should I send Andy a thank you note?' We laugh together for a while and then settle back and go through all the papers.

As I thought, they show everything. All the information regarding the business, where it states that I am a shared owner/company secretary and in the main, shows the money that I put in that set the business up in the beginning. I think that my solicitor, Phil (my tummy tingles oddly) will be happy.

I'm surprised that I'm quite excited to see him, but I think that it's mainly because this time I'm not the bereaved, dumped wife but a confident, newly single woman who has everything in hand and doesn't look quite so beaten down.

After several G&T's and a lot of laughs, we ask Giovanni for the bill. I'm staying at Chrissie's tonight, so we just need to get a taxi and I can drive to work in the morning from there.

'I say-a, Meeces 'arper (Giovanni really is Italian, so his accent is genuine - unlike Julio/Tony's) is not-a my place-a to speak, but-a I think-a you 'usband is silly man, vary silly man. E leave-a a beautiful lady for what?' he waves his hands-a in the air and says, 'Pah, E nota welcome in my rest-au-rant-a ever again! You are always-a welcome.'

His son, Giovanni Junior (genuine name) comes over with the bill as we had requested it, Giovanni (senior) promptly slaps Giovanni Junior around the head and screws up the bill. He says something in Italian which I have no idea what it is but the son blushes, apologises to us and rushes off to the kitchen with Giovanni (senior) still shouting after him in his native tongue.

'No bill tonight. Is free. On 'ouse.' I can't believe his kindness and thank him sincerely.

'Grazie mille Giovanni!' (I'm not fluent in Italian, I looked it up once on Google Translate.) I stand and give him a huge hug and a kiss on each cheek. It's now his turn to blush and as we leave, he starts shouting again in Italian to poor Giovanni Junior. It's hard not to laugh, but I think his poor son is definitely not finding the funny side of the situation.

Chapter 15

It's time to see my solicitor. The last few days have been busy as I've had several estate agents in to value the house, so now I have a figure to give to Phil (tingly tummy again). Bloody hell, it can't just happen every time I say Phil (tingle – apparently it can).

I've had my shower and washed my hair. It's so easy to manage now it's been cut into such a lovely style and my makeup, although minimal, adds a lovely glow. I put on my white summer dress as we're having a lovely Indian summer day and some tan leather sandals. I add a chunky bracelet and I'm ready. All the paperwork is in my tote bag and I'm just about to leave when my phone beeps. It's a text from Chrissie.

"Sorry love, you're going to have to go alone. Been called in work for a crisis meeting about one of my clients. Can't talk. Will ring later. Good luck xx"

"Don't worry. Hope all OK. Speak later xx"

I have a bit of a flutter in my stomach as I think about not having to share my appointment. Well, he is good looking, and I am only human.

I go back upstairs and put a little perfume on. Oh, don't read anything into it, I just happen to like it and wanted to smell nice for … erm … for myself.

I arrive about 15 minutes early so have time to still my beating heart and calm down. The snooty receptionist is on sentry duty and is giving me 'the evils' from her desk. Seriously, why do they have her in view of the public? I mean, if it wasn't for Chrissie making me the appointment I would have walked right out. She would look good as an interrogator flashing a torch in your eyes while shouting, 'Who are you? Who is your appointment with? TELL ME! TELL ME!!'

OK, definitely too many cop films. (She's bad cop in case you were wondering.) The gestapo stands and says "You vill follow me" – maybe not with the wartime German accent but still…

Phil stands and grins and says (which took me by surprise) 'Wow, you look amazing!" His eyes widen as he realises what he's said - in front of Hitler no less - and he blushes, actually blushes! It's so cute, I can't help but smile, well until I realise the giant beside me is staring open mouthed and fuming. I mean, I can feel the anger coming off her (me thinks someone has a little crush). Anyway, can't a man give a woman a bloody compliment without the world stopping and everyone going into freeze frame? I guess not.

'You vant tea!' she tells me. 'No thank you.' I reply (silently adding 'Mein Fuhrer' to the end). So immature, but who cares? And then, thankfully, she's gone and I'm left smiling at Phil ready to get down to business.

'So, I've got ...' I say at the same time Phil says, 'So, did you ...'

'Sorry you first,' he says at the same time as I say, 'Sorry you first.'

I'm blushing like a ripe tomato but thankfully so is he, when horror of horrors, he gets up and walks out of the room. Oh my God. What do I do? What did I say? Do I leave?

While my brain works at a mile a minute, I hear a knock at the door.

'Come in?' I say and Phil walks in, smiles and holds his hand out for me to shake.

'Hello, I'm Phil and I specialise in Marital law and awkward situations. Which can I help you with today?' He's sits down at his desk and smiles.

'I think I'll go with marital law today thank you, awkward situations I'm quite good at.' I laugh and with that, the tension is broken.

We get down to business and the reason he's been in touch. He had received a letter from Andy's solicitor. Apparently, because Andy was leaving the country with BZ (I can't even be bothered to say her name now) he would like the divorce to go ahead as quickly as possible.

Therefore, he was asking if I would divorce him on the grounds of adultery and he would cover the costs. His offer still stood with the house and pensions, but he had made no offer on the business.

I show Phil the documents that I had in my possession and point out where it states that I am Company Secretary and that it was my inheritance that started the business.

'How did you manage to get all this information?' He looks stunned but pleased to have all the facts to hand.

'Well, if I told you I'd have to kill you and where would that leave us?' He laughs good heartedly at my feeble joke and says deadpan, 'We do have a very good criminal defence solicitor too.'

'It's a long, embarrassingly funny story and one that will only be told after several bottles of wine.'

'Maybe I need to take you up on that, obviously on a professional basis.' *Is he flirting?* 'I mean your story sounds very intriguing and I hope to hear it one day, but don't forget lawyer/client confidentiality means I won't tell another soul. After all, I am a professional.' He grins, and it does funny things to my insides.

'Well, it's a kind offer but we'll leave that until the next date,' I laugh and then realise what I had said. 'Date? Did I say date? I meant appointment, ha ha silly me.' The laugh that follows is high pitched and my red face gives away my embarrassment. It's been so long since anyone flirted with me and at the first one I turn into a hysterical gibbering wreck.

Thankfully, after that, the rest of the appointment runs fine, and I agree that I am more than happy to divorce my snivelling ratbag of a husband under whatever grounds he wants. As for the issue with the business, Phil says he needs to read through all the documents and he will write to Andy's solicitor and ask him to get the business valued. He also tells me to get a couple of valuations too, and as company secretary I'm quite entitled to do so. He says he's going to draw up the divorce documents, but it would be easier if the financial situation was dealt with first.

Before I know it, it's time for me to go and with another shake of the hand (and a tingle or two) I go to leave.

'Amanda, I hope you don't mind me saying this,' *oh god have I got food in my teeth? Is my zip down?* Thankfully, he can't read my mind. 'But, you do look lovely. I don't mean that you didn't look nice before because erm … well you did, I mean ... Oh, I'm bloody rubbish at this!' He takes a deep breath and says, 'You look more in control and the new look suits you AND I hope I've not overstepped the mark by saying that.'

'Oh wow, right … erm no, not at all, thank you.' I leave his office grinning like a bloody teenager. *I look lovely!*

'LEAVE?' Chrissie shouts down the phone. 'Is that all you said, bloody *thank you* and then you left?'

'Actually, I believe I said 'Oh wow' too. Anyway, what did you expect me to do? Grab him and jump him on his desk?' (Not that the thought has gone through my head ... much).

'No of course not.' she grumbles. 'It just feels wrong to leave it like that.'

'Erm Hello! I'm not sure you know this, but I'm going through a divorce and am very vulnerable right now. My husband has left me for young hottie, and now I'm having to re-think my whole bloody life and mooning over my 'divorce solicitor' does seem a bit wrong somehow, don't you think?' I take a deep breath.

'Well, if you're going to put it like that of course it sounds wrong.' She's doing her grumpy voice and I hear her take another drink and then she sighs, 'What can I say? I'm sorry love, I can't help it. I'm just an old fuckin' romantic.' We both laugh at that as she's anything but.

'He's my solicitor, albeit a gorgeous one but he could be married, have a girlfriend, be gay…' Not that I believe the last one but still. 'and I'm seeing him again next week, so I'll tell you what he says next time. He's going to ring me when he hears anything and I'm leaving it at that OK?'

'O-kaay', she reluctantly agrees. We say goodnight and I hang up the phone (well I don't physically hang up, I just press the red button, but I'm old school). I ask myself the question that is going around my mind. Would I like to see Phil outside of his role in my divorce? I'm intrigued to know what he's like without his suit on. I don't mean like that! I meant does he wear jeans? Chino's? Nothing?... oh ahem, I guess I did mean it like that. Does he have hairy legs? Is he muscly? What are his feet like? (What? Imagine if he had athletes foot and extra-long toenails. It's important to know these things.)

Anyway, back to the original question. The simple answer is yes, I would, but the complicated answer is not yet. I'm just getting over a monumental change in my life and now is not the right time to jump into anything, even with someone as lovely as he is.

(I wonder if he has a hairy chest?)

Chapter 16

The following weeks are a mixture of work, (I've gone back part-time), sorting through the house and separating things as best as I can. It's not been easy, and I've had a few setbacks, one when I came across our wedding album and another when I found the box of pictures and cards that the children had drawn growing up; Just birthday and Christmas stuff really, but they all said, 'To Mummy and Daddy' and that set me off again.

The worst 'melt down' was when I found the box of family photographs; albums holding pictures of us all together, from our teenage years onwards. Memories caught on camera. Our smiling faces at the births of our children. Birthdays, holidays, Christmas, each photograph another small fracture in my heart. How does someone throw it all away, like rubbish in the bin? Toss it all aside for a pretty face. I cry for a little while, but these were the hardest things to face in the big 'sort out', and I've done it now and survived. Puffy eyes heal, the heart will take a little longer.

I must admit, it is slowly getting easier as the time goes on. This is my life now and I have 2 choices - I can either crumble (which periodically I do), or I can stand tall and start again, naturally I choose the latter.

I met with Phil a few days ago and it was purely professional. There were no awkward moments or silly blushes. In fact, he said he was going away for a couple of weeks and if I had any problems I was to ring his secretary. I asked if he was going anywhere nice, (why do we ask that? Like you'd intentionally go on holiday to somewhere dreadful!) but he said it was just the usual place. I was about to enquire further (yes, I am nosey), but his phone rang, and the moment passed. Maybe he is married. Anyway, tingles aside, I remained calm and demure and we agreed to meet in a few weeks as we were still waiting for the valuations on the business.

I hear Chrissie's car pull up. She's here to help me sort through my clothes. Andy's was easy as I just pulled everything out of the drawers and wardrobes and threw them into bags and had left them in the garage weeks ago. But I didn't realise I had so many clothes, and I know that I'll never wear some of them again. To be honest they're bloody awful! My wardrobe was just full of dark trousers and long skirts, tunics and cardigans. Most of my clothes were from M&S as it was a nice comfortable option, but Chrissie said, 'Comfort is a fuckin' fabric softener, which you are not!' I have to agree she made a good point, so she is here to empty my wardrobe of O.A.P. clothing.

She's let herself in as usual and has thoughtfully brought a bottle of wine. I've got a chicken in the oven and I plan on making sandwiches later so the wine will be lovely with it. Or, for a more realistic version, the wine will be gone before the chicken is cooked and the bottle I bought for this evening will then have to be opened. Oh, life can be hard sometimes.

One hour in and I'm realising just how hard life *can* be. Chrissie has virtually emptied my wardrobe. My comfortable shoes have gone. My comfortable trousers have gone (except my new ones as they don't have elasticated waistbands), my comfortable tunics, my comfortable cardigans, the first bottle of wine … all gone.

'Mandy love, what the hell is this?' she holds up a pleated kilt in a red tartan pattern. 'Maybe, if it was 3 inches shorter you could wear it with some dark tights and knee-high boots but fuck me it's shocking! Did you ever go shootin' in the wee highlands?'

'Actually, that was Andy's.' I say blushing. We stare at each other and then the skirt and then each other again and then hysterical laughing starts, I think the wine is working its magic.

'Ahahaha oh…my…god…why?'

'Did he have a sporran too? hahahaha'

'Did he wear underwear? Hahahaha'

A wedding, yes and HELL YES, were my answers between laughing and opening the second bottle of wine, followed by retrieving the burnt chicken from the oven, which now looks like the someone ate the flesh and put the skin back in a vague chicken shape. At least the skin was nice and crispy.

We settle for some cheese on toast and then carry all 6 bags of clothes and shoes to the front door, ready to load in the car in the morning.

By the time we've done all that and finished the rest of the wine (obviously), we chill in the living room with our feet up. We settle on watching a rom com about an American woman who goes to propose to her boyfriend in Ireland because the dope hasn't done it yet. But, she has to travel across Ireland with this gorgeous bloke, who she hates (spoiler alert – she really doesn't), in a crappy car and … Don't worry, I won't ruin the ending for you. Anyway, when it finishes I find that it's not me that's crying as per usual, but Chrissie – I would like to point out that this never happens. Ever. I think she would be stoned in her home town or something for crying over some soppy chick flick. But needless to say, she is and doesn't seem to be stopping.

'Oh my God, what wrong?' I ask. I'm in unknown territory and don't know what to do as she has never cried in front of me. Not even during her divorces. Me? I'm usually like Gwyneth Paltrow on Oscar night.

'I can help, if you tell me.' Please let me be able to help, if she tells me.

'Oh God!' she wails. *Oh God*, I think, maybe I can't help her.

She takes a deep breath and then tells me she's been seeing Simon and it's been going great. Now, I've obviously been here with Chrissie a couple of times, but I can honestly say this is the first man to make her cry before the wedding. Obviously, this one is an utter bastard but better she finds out now rather than later.

'You're better off without him love, he was obviously a bad one to begin with.'

'What the fuck are you on about?' she sniffs and blows her nose, quite loudly, on the tissue I handed her.

'Well, erm … I'm not sure now, but if he's making you cry already love that's not a, erm … well it's not a good thing now, is it?' I try to reason with her with my best counselling voice. I usually have far less erm's when I'm in professional mode though.

'No! I like him, a lot, and I think he likes me.'

'Huh?' Now I'm really confused. I must have drunk more wine that I thought.

'Well, he seems to like me, and we have so much in common, but oh fuck, what if he changes his mind? I don't want him to and I have no idea what I'll do if he does. Is this what it's like being you?' (Ouch, that one hurt but I'll let it go as she's obviously distressed, and possibly a little drunk.) She blows her nose again on another tissue and I hand her the box as I'm getting repetitive strain injury from constantly reaching for a clean one for her. I'm genuinely dumbfounded and I have no words. In fact, I'm doing a marvellous impression of a fish as I just keep opening my mouth to say something and closing it again when I realise it was just rubbish.

'Isn't this where you give me some sound advice or something?' she asks, looking at me wide eyed.

Bloody hell, is this what I've been like?

'Well … panda eyes are so last year love.' I say, at least I managing to raise a smile from her. 'It seems to me that you've found someone who makes you feel good and who you feel an equal to and you're scared to death of losing him. Is that right?'

'Yeees.' She wails, her large moon like eyes are back, filled with unshed tears.

'Why don't you just take a step back, relax and enjoy the ride.' (Hark at me! Enjoy the ride, indeed.) 'If what you're saying about Simon is right, then he's a good guy. Look at all the effort he went to convincing you that he was sorry for his stupid remark. He didn't need to bother doing that, so maybe he thinks you're worth it.' Chrissie takes a big sniff and wipes her nose and eyes and under her chin where the tears were meeting and dripping with astounding regularity.

'You think so?' she asks. *I bloody hope so.*

'I know so.' I say. Chrissie takes a deep breath and I give her a huge cuddle.

'Thanks, Mand. I love ya, you know.' She nudges me with her elbow.

'I love you too, you soppy cow!' I nudge her back and we both reach for the wine. Unfortunately, it seems we have almost finished the second bottle, red cooking wine here we come.

Chapter 17

Its late September now and the weather has started to cool down for Autumn, but the odd sunny day pops up here and there. English weather is unpredictable to say the least – it can snow in May and be warm enough in December that you don't even need a coat.

I still receive messages from all my new friends in the South, and they ask when I'm going back. John needs help with the pub quiz and Mary say's Julio was devastated to think I wasn't going back to Salsa.

I must confess to missing them all so much too, but surprisingly I also miss being on the coast. Just listening to the sound of the sea was soothing, even on the most treacherous days when the ocean waves were crashing on the shore, it brought a calm that I can't explain. The air just felt clearer or maybe that's just my head. Either way

I do know that I have a lot of thinking to do about my future. I need to talk to my mum and Mike and see what they think. I'll ring them and arrange to go down for a few days. It'll be lovely to spend some time with them plus, as a bonus, I love where they live in Tenby.

The fact is, I only have Chrissie here and if things work out with Simon she'll be busy herself. My children are flung all over the UK, so there isn't really anything keeping me here. I decide another trip to see the area is a must and being the spontaneous lady whom I have now become, I message Audrey and Terry to see when the cottage is available. We agree on two weeks' time.

I've spoken to the children about everything that's happening with me and their dad and they are in full support. They know about the business and the house and the grounds of the divorce and all three of them are mad at their dad, but I've told them that's not what I want. Regardless of them being grown up he's still their dad and they shouldn't have to take sides. I just wanted them to be in the picture with what's happening.

Ellie was the one most upset, as I knew she would be. She was always a daddy's girl and is struggling so much with the whole thing, but thankfully she talks to me about it which is good. Jackie was working all weekend, so Ellie came to stay for a couple of days. We had a lovely time reminiscing, crying and laughing at old photographs. I hear it's the best medicine.

I decide not to tell Ellie, or the others about my dabble in espionage; it doesn't look good knowing that their mum is potentially a criminal.

After spending ages wanting Andy to contact me, unfortunately he did when he found out that I'd taken the files. He wasn't happy and threw a huge wobbler. I think his language would have made Chrissie blush and that's saying something.

On the advice of my solicitor (and Chrissie, who 'flipped her lid' and said she would do unmentionable things to his unmentionables, if he ever spoke to me like that again), I wasn't to answer any more calls from Andy, so instead I've saved all the text messages and voicemail. But honestly? I'm getting a bit angry now. He chose to leave me for a 'young bloody Australian Physiotherapist called bloody Zooey'! *I* didn't have a choice in that. He tore my world apart and suddenly I'm the bad guy? I don't think so mister. I can't even ring my husband (soon to be ex) of 28-sodding-years to talk about what he would like from the house because of the abuse I receive. The counsellor in me thinks it's because he's feeling guilty. The wife in me thinks he can go to hell!

Don't get me wrong, I'm not all tough Zena warrior princess, I'm still struggling with the fact that my life went from 'comfortable' (I'm beginning to hate that word now) and secure, to a mess in the space of just a few hours. One day I'm happily married and the next I'm on the road to an acrimonious divorce.

It's been about 6 months now since he left and overall, I'm OK and have been taking positive steps to move forward. The business got valued, along with the house, pensions, shares, savings etc. I've been seeing my solicitor a fair bit and on a professional level only, but I still get a bit tingly when I see him. Well, I'm only human, and he is a very handsome man and I dare anyone to be in a room with him and not feel a little flutter, especially when he's in his Navy Armani Suit and blue shirt with the cufflinks just showing beneath his jacket sleeve, or his crisp white shirt with the top button undone and his tie loosened slightly, and his shirt sleeves rolled up to show his Patek Philippe watch and hairy forearms … ahem, anyway I'm sure you know what I mean.

He's been a little distant with me lately, or maybe it's my imagination? He's probably just being professional. There have been no further flirty episodes, so I think it was more wishful thinking on my part, but a girl can still ~~drool~~ dream.

The financial agreement has been drawn up and I can now see why Andy didn't want me to get my hands on the paperwork I'd acquired. But, being the reasonable sap that I am, I photocopied everything and sent copies back to him, albeit a few weeks later. At least that way he would have the same information to give to his solicitor which would speed up the whole process, and I did steal them in the first place.

I'm trying to get used to the changes in my life, but knowing Andy's going home to BZ and having dinner with her and going to bed with her and having S.E.X. with her is still hard to deal with at times. Thankfully, the 'times' are coming less and less. (Hopefully he is too.)

'I miss sex!' I wailed to Chrissie when she popped round later that evening with the customary bottle of wine and an update on Phil's flirting or lack of flirting as the case is.

'I can't remember the last time I had it and knowing he's doing it all the time isn't helping.'

'Aww, I understand how hard that is.' she agrees kindly.

'No, you don't!' I grumble at her as she's positively glowing. 'You're bonking Simon all the time and I can see that smug 'I've just been shagged' look about you.'

'You're right, I am, I have, and I plan to do so again later.' She grins at me. 'I was just trying to be supportive and agree with you. And since when did you start using words like bonked and shagged? Just for the record, no one uses the words bonk, bonked or bonking any more. I think the kids call it 'dusting' nowadays. Flamin' idiots!' She rolls her eyes and I can't help but smile.

'Well, call it what you want but I dust this house regularly and I think I'd know if I came across a penis on the mantelpiece!' We laugh together. 'Why am I laughing? I'm still not having any sex and I know after 33 years we had slowed it down to maybe once a week, or a fortnight, or a... well it doesn't matter because the point is I was still having *some* sex and now I'm not and do you want to know what's worse? Well I'll tell you anyway, it's knowing that Andy is. No doubt regularly as she's younger, fitter, better looking than I'll ever be, and she hasn't had three children, doesn't have stretch marks and I'll bet she's got perky boobs too just to naff me off!' My chest is heaving from my outburst. Blimey, where did that come from?

'Wow, I think that's the first proper rant I've heard from you. Well done love.' She raises her glass and smiles. 'It's about time you had a rant about the bastard.

Oh, don't give me that look, I always swear, it's like second-fuckin'-nature. See? I can't even help it.' She gives me a wink and squeezes my hand. 'Right, what we need love, is a plan. "Operation Shag Mandy"!' Chrissie announced.

I laugh at the ridiculousness of it. I may miss it but having sex with someone other than Andy scares the living daylight out of me. For starters I'll have to get rid of the Wookie look again (what can I say? It's trouser season).

'Oh God, I'll have to let someone see me naked.'

'Yep, that's usually the idea but I have heard that there's a thing the kids do, and it's called "dry humping". Apparently, the kids keep their clothes on but rub their bodies on each other and get off that way.   Sounds like a total waste of a shag to me but I guess it cuts down on teenage pregnancy.' I hold my head in my hands. How do I start all that again?

'Look, I'm not saying it'll be easy love,' Chrissie continues, ignoring my obvious discomfort and swiftly passing the tissues as my eyes have started to leak. I'm not crying, I'm just leaking. 'If you overthink it you'll never do it and you'll become celibate, like a eunuch only the female version, a eunuch-ess.'

'I don't think that's an actual word and I'm not just going to have sex with anybody!'

'What about if we go out clubbing and see what comes up. No pun intended.' She laughs at her own joke.

'I'm 47 Chrissie, I don't go clubbing!   And I don't have one-night stands if that's what you're thinking. I go to fancy bistro's and wine bars.' She gives me the look.

'Well I would if I went out but that's not the point. Bloody clubbing? As if!'

So naturally here I am, playing third wheel to Chrissie and Simon (who, it turns out is a genuinely nice guy) and queueing to get into a nightclub called Destiny.

It took me ages to decide what to wear (I mean what do people actually wear to clubs these days?). Chrissie put up with my utter panic and after several days of whining (her not me), I end up buying a silver sparkly vest top and a black pencil skirt and team them with my Jimmy Choo's. I'm not thrilled at the idea of clubbing, especially when I see the line of people queueing to get in. It feels like every woman has looked me up and down several times, which does little to boost my confidence, and they all look young enough to be any one of my kids, which does even less for my confidence. Can this night get any more embarrassing?

Apparently so.

'Hi Mrs Daniels!' shouts the bouncer, aka Daniel the security guard from our building. 'Come through.' The queue of men and women, or should I say lads and lasses, and a few ladette's too, all grumble at our priority treatment. I'm blushing so much I'm lighting the way, like Florence Nightingale and her lamp, and Chrissie is laughing at them all and doing a royal wave, which only seems to involve waving two fingers in a circular motion at everyone. Oh no, now it's just one finger. Please kill me now.

Once we're in I can't hear anything. Chrissie is moving her mouth. Then Simon is. Then Chrissie. I stare open mouthed at them both. Then Chrissie does the universal "want a drink?" hand gesture, and I confirm, quite animatedly to say I'm only nodding, that indeed I do. Hopefully I can be forgiven for holding up my two fingers in what may be construed as a rude gesture, when I just meant, would it be possible for you to get me two beverages please instead of just the one?

They both go to the bar and I'm left looking around the place and I'm happy to see now that it's a mixture of ages and I'm not the oldest one here. In fact, the white-haired chap in the bow tie and obvious toupee is holding the title for "Oldest Rocker". He must be sweltering under that rug. I'm sure it must be like wearing a woolly hat on a summers day.

The music is good, with a range of 80's to noughties, but it's just so loud, and I've listened to three songs while I've been waiting for our drinks as the bar was heaving. You could die of thirst in here (and go deaf).

I'm swaying along nicely to the music when a guy nudges me and moves his mouth.

'yboijiodjl'

'What?' I mouth.

'yboijiodjl', he tries again.

'What?' I mouth again, and he tries again, and again, and again! Bloody hell, I've got to give him credit, he's persistent if nothing else.

The music quietens to a level where I can just make out his 7th attempt. 'YOU'RE BEAUTIFUL!' I can't believe that he has spent all that time saying, 'you're beautiful' over and over again. I wonder at what point would he have given up? I smile at him, say thank you and am worrying about what to say when lucky for me Chrissie and Simon appear with the drinks and I, rudely I must admit, say sorry and turn my back on the poor guy. He taps my shoulder, and Chrissie leans around me and tells him, in no uncertain terms to 'Piss Off!'

'SORRY ABOUT THAT. IT TOOK FUCKIN' AGES!' Chrissie shouts above the noise so I can just about hear her. 'SEEN ANYONE WORTH SHAGGING YET?' Unfortunately, the music had quietened down just at the same moment she bellowed the last sentence and funnily enough I'm getting quite a lot of looks my way now.

Chrissie is oblivious as she's bouncing around to the music with Simon. I just feel like a spare part, and one that apparently is eager to have sex. Through my cringing I can see her eyeing up the talent for me, of which I've seen none yet.

I'm on my second drink as I see someone's arm waving and trying to push through the crowd, but I can't see who it's attached to. I look around me for the recipient of the wave and can't see anyone waving back. The arm is getting closer and then, through the crowd, a familiar face appears. Well, I would never have put him in a place like this (ignoring the fact that I am, in fact, in this place).

'PHIL!'

'I WOULD NEVER HAVE PUT YOU IN A PLACE LIKE THIS!' He shouts at me.

'I WAS JUST THINKING THE SAME ABOUT YOU.'

'WHAT?'

I try again but it's so noisy in here that all I can hear is a drum beat in my ears along with a terrible ringing. (God, I feel old.) He gestures for me to follow him, to what I hope is a quieter part of the club. I look at him in his 'own clothes' and not his office 'uniform'. The jeans he's wearing hug his bottom quite nicely and teamed with a white fitted shirt tucked in and finished off with a tan leather belt and shoes, he looks more gorgeous than normal.

'Fancy seeing you in here.' He says in a normal voice as we've found the only quiet place in the club, or should I say outside the club, in the smoking section. I hide my distaste and pray he's not going to light up in front of me. I'm not a smoker and didn't picture Phil as one either.

'Sorry, but this seemed the only quiet place in the club, youlooklovelybytheway.' He says the last part in such quick succession to his previous statement that I almost miss it. Is he nervous? He runs his hand through his hair and smiles at me in a slightly sheepish way. 'What brings you here?' he asks. Well, I can't tell him it's because I miss sex and my best friend is trying to find me a one-night stand, can I?

'I'm playing gooseberry to Chrissie and Simon, her new fella. It's great fun.' I deadpan, hoping it's a good explanation. 'What about you?'

'Stag party. My younger brother is getting married, so I've been dragged here by him and his mates. I must admit, it's not my choice of night out. I can't stand being somewhere that you're required to endure passive smoking just to have a conversation. I also realise that I sound like an old man and am probably digging myself a huge hole here.'

I laugh easily. 'Don't be silly. I'm fully in agreement with you. My ears are ringing, I can't hear what anyone is saying in there and it looks so rude when I keep shouting WHAT? PARDON and CAN YOU SAY THAT AGAIN?'

Now at this point I'm feeling that the evening is starting to improve. I can feel myself relaxing, although that could be the effects of the marijuana the guy next to us is smoking (isn't it illegal or something?) when Chrissie and Simon appear.

'Phil!' she shouts and envelopes him in a great big hug. He smiles easily and hugs her back, shaking hands with Simon after he's been introduced. He is simply gorgeous to watch and has a smile that would melt the most hardened heart.

'So, what are you doing sneaking off with our Mand? Not up to anything naughty, are you?' She asks Phil as she waggles her eyebrows in a 'Benny Hill' kind of way. Oh God please take me now. Phil blushes and looks totally uncomfortable but before he can say anything a younger guy comes over, puts his arm around Phil's shoulders and shouts, 'Bro, where have you been? It's your round!' The similarity is striking from the bright blue eyes to the easy smile.

'Give me a minute Pete and I'll be right with you.' He turns back to me smiling but the mood, if there ever was one, has gone as his brother is smiling at me too and still has him arm firmly around Phil's shoulders.

They cut a funny pair and I can't help but laugh. 'Off you go. I'll see you again soon no doubt.' I am secretly deflated knowing he's going but his brother's stag party obviously comes first. 'Congratulations on your wedding!' I say to Pete and they both leave me and disappear in a cloud of cigarette and marijuana smoke.

'Well Mrs Darkhorse, what was going on there?' Chrissie is asking but I'm fully dejected and feel the need for a long shower and a lung transplant.

'Nothing.' It's true really. Nothing was going on. Has he asked me out for a drink? No. Has he made any other move other than to say I look nice? No. I think that I'm reading far too much into it and I'm tired. 'I'm going home and please don't argue with me.' I say as they start to argue with me. 'I'm just tired and my head's banging. You two soppy sods can now finish your night on the dancefloor and I no longer have to play gooseberry to two mooning lovebirds.'

After a couple of feeble attempts to make me stay, they respect my need for my nice comfy bed and make sure I'm put safely in a taxi, carefully selected from the 20 others waiting outside the club. This taxi driver had a nice face according to Chrissie, but as you never can tell, she's entered the taxi number and registration plate into her phone and told the poor man exactly that while taking a picture of him. 'So, no funny business or I'll find you and you won't be fuckin' happy if I do!' I'm sure he mumbled something which sounded like "I'm not fuckin' happy now' but I can't be certain due the tinnitus ringing in my ears.

'I'LL RING YOU TOMORROW!' I shout, and wave at them both as the taxi pulls away. Once we're around the corner I apologise profusely to the poor driver and tip him excessively for what was a relatively short journey.

After closing the front door, I burst into tears.

(I seem to do this a lot.)

Chapter 18

'Right, well we're just going to have to go with plan B.' says Chrissie. She called the next day to check I was OK. I didn't tell her about my melt down when I got home.

'Plan B? I didn't know we had one.'

'There's always a Plan B and in your case, it's going to mean another shopping trip but this time it's one with a difference.' She's grinning at me in a scarily salacious manner.

'Why are you looking at me like that?' She's doing a very good impression of a sex offender.

Her reply of 'you'll see' didn't put me at ease, and I found out why half an hour later when we pull up outside a sex shop, albeit a high street one.

'No way.' I say, sitting in the car with my arms folded and a look on my face that shows, in no uncertain terms, the chances of me getting out of the car.

Sadly, the odds were stacked against me when she threatened to bring any items she thought I might need to the door and waggle them around shouting *"Is this the one you mean?"*

'I can't believe you made me come here.' I hiss at her as we go downstairs to the specialist section, to which her reply was 'No love, it's to make you come later,' and bursts out laughing. She is absolutely loving this.

My mind is boggled at the selection of phallic objects that may or may not require 3 AAA batteries. The conscientious shop assistant comes over and asks if she can help.

'No thank you.' I say, as Chrissie says, 'Yes please.'

The poor girl doesn't know which one of us to go to, but I assume she's on commission, so she naturally chooses Chrissie.

'My friend is recently divorced and in need of a 'little attention', if you know what I mean and I'm just wondering whether she should start off with something small or go the whole hog and get something a little special, that will sing to her and make her breakfast in the morning.' Chrissie and the sales assistant are laughing out loud at her humour and I am dying with embarrassment. I turn away to hide my embarrassment and turn smack into a rack of rubberised male appendages. It wobbles but I manage to grab it before we're standing in a sea of latex willies. I leave Chrissie to talk to the shop assistant as she seems to know more about my sexual needs that I do.

'What about a bullet?' Good Lord will this torture never end? I look at the floor and moved further away but when I look up I find I'm now stood in the middle of the torture section, how apt. I'm facing a wall of PVC bodysuits, corsets and matching knickers. There's also some paddle shaped thing (like a table tennis bat), handcuffs and blindfolds amongst everything.

Thankfully there's a lingerie section and I've spotted a very nice lacy number (I don't know why they don't sell this upstairs as I'm sure more people would buy it), so feeling more confident I stride over. It looks like a nice all-in-one lace body, I pick up one in my size and hold it up for further inspection, but that's when I see that there are slots for the nipples and err lower bits to stand out. I can tell you one thing, there's not a stitch of support in it and there's more chance of my nipples standing out of the crotch bit. I hastily push it back onto the rail.

'Are you checking out stuff to wear for Phil,' Chrissie shouts over to me. Sometimes I think she doesn't know me at all, or she just loves embarrassing me. 'Anyway, come over here and check this out.' She shows me something called a Rabbit. Appropriately named, I can see bunny ears, but I've never seen them attached to a rather large penis.

I am shown so many different 'Rabbit's' that my mind is boggled. There's the Original, The Purple Silicone Curved one, The Bendy one, The Metal one (ouch), The Morgasm Move Rechargeable one and, going off the price, the king of all 'Rabbit's'- The Luxury Rechargeable

Rabbit Vibrator at a whopping £189! I know it's not always easy to achieve an orgasm but for that price I'd want a weekend away thrown in.

Just to end the torture I agree to buy 'The Original' (it's on sale) and the wonderfully helpful shop assistant throws in a 'Bullet' (as she has one and has never looked back).

'Lovely, thank you, goodbye.' I mumble and virtually run out the shop. I'm sure her parting words of 'come again' were said just to embarrass me further. How are they able to talk so openly about such intimate stuff? I mean, I know Chrissie really well, but I have never, EVER, talked about anything like this with her before. And the fact that the young shop assistant (did I not mention she only looked about 18?) had a fully open conversation about the differences in climaxing with a rabbit or a bullet.

I am not feeling any better knowing that I've spent over £50 and somehow must work out how to return the items without having to come to the shop ever again.

'I don't know what you're grumbling about!' Chrissie and I have been arguing all the way back to the house.

'It was so embarrassing. That young girl looked at me like I'm some middle aged desperate divorcee who can't get a man so has to use a toy to get some attention.'

'Wow, she was good if one look gave you that whole impression.' Chrissie smiles at me. 'I'm not arguing with you, but you need to loosen up love. I get that you don't want a one-night stand. Neither would I to be honest, but this way you get to have a little fun, at your own pace and without worrying if he's going to respect you in the morning.'

I agree, begrudgingly, that she has a point, but I'll think about it and if I want a refund of the fur-free bunny Chrissie will take it back for me.

'Hoo-fuckin'-ray!' she shouts. 'Now with all that talk of climaxes and stimulation, I'm going home to get me some lovin'!' That is a mental image I wish I didn't have.

We say goodbye and I'm left standing on my drive, with my embarrassing items in a bright purple bag, that has the name of the store splashed all over. It took me over an hour to stop blushing and over a week just to open the bag, which I'd hid in the back of my wardrobe in case I had visitors and they found it. (Odd visitors I know.)

Now ladies, regarding the bullet - I'm not saying that you should all dump your husbands/boyfriends/wives/ girlfriends etc but, you really do need to invest in one of these babies.

Enough said.

Chapter 19

It's Autumn and Halloween has been and gone along with the fireworks celebrating Bonfire Night, although it should be called Bonfire month as the fireworks seem to go on for weeks. I know it isn't everyone's favourite season as it obviously marks the end of the lighter nights and warm days, but I just love the darker evenings and autumn leaves.

From being small it was always my favourite season. Snuggled up indoors with my mum and dad playing board games and reading. There wasn't a 24-hour kid's channel on the TV or internet and mobile phones to distract us from wanting to play and use our imaginations.

Even when my children were little I would make sure we did things as a family and encouraged them to play together. Granted it didn't always work and there was a fair few squabbles between them, but I hope that they look back on it with the same fondness I do. I always think that we are adults a long time, so children should get to keep their innocence and eagerness to play as long as possible. I know I'm a soppy beggar, but I do miss those times.

As the season moved on, thankfully so did I. The terrible clubbing experience and embarrassing trip to Ann Summers were safely behind me. Obviously, one turned out to be more positive than the other but there's no need to get into that right now.

Today has been a difficult day. One of my clients came to see me because her child had recently died. Nathanial was only 4 when he was diagnosed with leukaemia and he lost his battle after just 2 years. Karen is married and has two other beautiful, and healthy, children but the loss of Nathanial has naturally been hard on them all. Listening to this poor woman cry and talk, it took me all my strength not to cry myself.

By the time the hour session ended we were both emotionally fraught and I just felt drained and in desperate need for a long soak in the bath with a glass of wine and my Marian Keyes novel.

Unfortunately, that was not the worst part of my day. When I got home from work there was a large envelope on the mat. When I saw the franking stamp from my solicitor I knew instantly what it would be. My divorce papers and financial agreement had arrived and although I knew this day would come, it's still like a blow to the chest. All I need to do is sign on the dotted line and hey presto, in a couple of months I'll be divorced. 28 years, gone in a signature. I know I'm simplifying it, but that's how it feels. I'm numb, like I'm watching my life from afar. Sounds are muffled around me. The radio is playing something that sounds familiar, but I can't remember what.

I look outside and see people driving past, walking past, all wrapped up against the cold evening wind. Are they happy? Sad? Who knows? None of them know that I'm stood in here, about to end my marriage with a flick of a pen. I wonder whether Andy is feeling the same or whether he's jumping for joy with BZ.

I know I'm torturing myself but it's so hard not to. And now there's the whole subject of what I call myself. Do I go back to being called Miss? I feel a bit old for that and as for being a Ms, well naturally I'm too young for that (I am!). Is there a middle ground? Could it not be Missy? Misee? Mizee? God, they all sound terrible AND I'm going to have to revert to my maiden name, Markham. It's not a bad name but Missy Mandy Markham is a bit of a mouthful. I think I'll ponder that one with Chrissie when I get back from my trip to Cornwall with a slight diversion to see Mum and Mike.

It seems so long since I've seen mum, I'm ashamed to admit it was well before all this divorce stuff. I know I should have gone sooner but I couldn't face her. I feel that I've let her down somehow as I couldn't hold onto my husband and I've brought shame to the family. I know I sound like I'm in Downton Abbey, but mum and dad were with each other from school and that's all I wanted and what I had. But now, I'm going to be a divorcee. It just doesn't feel like that's what my life should be like. All my adult life I've been either a girlfriend, fiancée, wife, mum and now grandma, and to be single just makes me feel like I'm freefalling without a parachute. I really don't know how to be just Amanda Markham. I guess I have no choice now except to find out.

Anyway, back to reality first on the agenda is my luxurious soak in the bath with my new bath bomb, obviously not forgetting the wine and my book. Then I'll sort out packing for my visit to Tenby.

One thing this divorce has done is made me travel more. OK, I know I've only been to Devon and now Tenby, but I would never have dreamt of doing that before. Andy did all the driving if we went anywhere. It just became the natural pattern that he would walk towards the driver's door and me towards the passenger door. But, now that it's just me and the driver's door, well it's a whole new world!

I set off with no drama this time and I put my music on, sing out of tune to my heart's content and just take in the beautiful scenery. Kenny and Dolly all the way.

Mum and Mike live in a beautiful bungalow overlooking Tenby harbour. It's gorgeous there with its mixture of beautiful pastel coloured houses with old Georgian buildings mixed amongst fisherman's cottages. I don't know why I don't come here more often (which is what I always say when I come here) it's just so pretty (which is also what I always say).

As I approach their home, I see Mike looking out of the lounge window, waving frantically the minute he sees me. You'd think I was his own daughter the way he is. He never had children of his own and I know he thinks of me as his substitute daughter, or maybe just his daughter.

Either way, he's a lovely man and I'm so happy that mum found someone after we lost dad. I'll confess, it was a bit hard at first knowing that mum had met someone. Dad had been gone 3 years, but it was still as raw to me as if he had died just the day before. But, I had to be grown up about it as I wasn't a child anymore. I was a mum and needed to act like one. So, naturally I sulked for weeks and refused to acknowledge him.

It's so embarrassing now when I think back to how rude I was. Mike and mum were so patient, but in the end, it was mum who just said 'Dad's gone love and if I could change that I would but I'm still here, living and breathing and finding my way and now I've been lucky enough to find someone I care about, who cares about me too. So, put your bloody face straight and start acting like the woman I raised and not the child you're being!' And that was that.

'Amanda! You look lovely,' flusters Mike as he opens my car door. 'How was the drive? Are you tired? Oh, you must be, it's such a long journey. We've missed you so much, haven't we Reeny?' Mum's name is Irene, but he insists on calling her that and to be honest it does suit her.

'Bloody hell Mike, give the girl a chance to get out of the car! Now move out of the way so I can give my baby girl a cuddle and tell her how much we've missed her.' She winks at me as she admonishes Mike for being a mother hen and I notice mum's using a stick and limping and she didn't have that before.

'Mum! What's the matter? Have you hurt yourself? Are you OK?'

'Good grief girl, now you sound like Mike. Let me answer at least one of your questions first. I'm OK, I took a fall a couple of months ago in the kitchen and my hip hasn't been right since. It's nothing serious, before you ask, just inflammation of the hip or something and I'm on some medication to sort it. Yes, I'm OK. Is that it? Any more questions?' She laughs after she's finished. 'Now, I'll bet you're parched, so let's have a brew and you can tell us all about that bastard of an ex-husband of yours!'

I guess I didn't need to be worried after all. Downton Abbey indeed.

It was so lovely to catch up. I told them all about Andy and his BZ and even about the heist, including all the planning and preparation, and both mum and Mike laughed until tears were rolling down their faces.

Unfortunately, that wasn't the only tearful part. Mum asked me if I really was OK and I said yes but then burst into tears. I think it was being with mum and knowing she'd always been there to pick me up when I fell, cuddle me when I was sad, and it was knowing that dad wasn't there to hug me either, but Mike is a pretty good substitute. So, basically, I was a snotty tearful mess for a while until I'd worn myself out, like a toddler after a tantrum.

We talked constantly until bedtime and all had an early night, although I think for them it's a normal night, and I slept better than I have in ages. I must have been more worried than I expected about telling mum. She gave me a good old telling off for worrying about letting her down and I must admit to feeling totally foolish once I'd said it out loud.

Mum's always been there for me, a friend as well as a mum and I count my blessings constantly as I know not everyone is as lucky. Mike, bless his heart, went out the morning after to give mum and me a chance to talk and catch up properly.

'How did you do it mum?' I asked as Mum was washing the breakfast pots and I was drying up. This always used to be the best time to talk to mum about 'girly stuff' and it felt right to do so now. It's a tried and tested method that works for us.

'Do what love?'

'How did you start your life over after dad died? Andy hasn't died but I can't see myself moving forward, I feel stuck in limbo.'

'When your dad died I thought I would never be able to breathe again, let alone have a life again. I felt as though I was slowly suffocating, and each breath just felt more and more of an effort. When I woke up in the mornings, for that split second, I'd forget he wasn't there and for that moment I felt peace. Then it would hit me, and it felt like someone was sat on my chest crushing me.'

We had both stopped what we were doing and when I looked at mum she was staring through the kitchen window at the garden, her face wet with tears.

'Oh mum, I'm so sorry. I didn't mean to get you upset.' I put my arms around her and we hugged.

'Don't be silly, I was just remembering that's all. I still miss your dad, but I'm lucky because I managed to fall in love twice and with two amazing men. I won't lie and say it was easy to move on, but it wasn't all bad. Gradually, over time, I would wake up and the feeling of peace started to last that little longer until eventually I was able to start living a little.'

We carried on doing the dishes when mum said, 'Starting over isn't easy. I had to learn how to be me again and not just a mum, wife or grandma. Find something that makes you happy and use that as your starting point. Try and remember the things that you used to do before married life took over.'

I was thinking about my drawing and painting and told mum about it. 'That's amazing sweetheart! You don't have to let the end of your marriage be the end of you. Think of it as a new beginning, that's all. I'm sure there were always parts of your life that you wish you'd handled differently, things you wished you'd pursued but didn't have the courage.

Well, now you do love. Make the most of it. It's not often we get to start again with a blank slate.' She returned to the task of washing up but had given me food for thought.

A new beginning eh? I liked the sound of that.

PART THREE

NEW BEGINNINGS

Chapter 20

My journey to Port Isaac from Tenby should have been a simple one, or so I thought. What I hadn't realised was that the Atlantic Ocean separated the two. I seem to have got into my head that the journey was just a little south of Tenby. As the crow flies it doesn't seem that bad, but the Atlantic Ocean had gotten in the way and split South Wales and Cornwall and the Bristol channel had joined in the fun. To top it off there was an accident on the M5 leaving Bristol and I was stuck there for over an hour, meaning that by the time we got moving at any decent speed, it was pouring down and the black clouds were rolling in threatening thunder and lightning for the rest of my journey, (I'm sure you can imagine how happy I was feeling.)

To say that I wanted to scream would be an understatement. To also say that I had forgotten to clip my phone in the little holder on the dash so that when it rang, while we were stationary on the motorway, I had to tip everything out over the passenger seat. Well, that was the icing on the cake. (I would never use my phone while driving, but we'd been sat for over an hour and I put it straight on 'hands free' officer).

'YES.' I shouted to the poor caller. I hadn't even looked who it was.

'Erm hi Amanda, it's Phil. Phil Harris, your solicitor. Is everything OK?'

'*Oh my God! It's Phil, It's Phil!*' My heart screamed at me. 'Behave woman, he's just your solicitor for goodness sake, act normal', my head countered.

'Amanda? Hello. Are you there?' Crap! I forgot he's still on the bloody phone.

'Oh, hiiii Phil. How ARE you?' What the hell was that? Where did my American accent come from? Oh God, now I'm blushing like a schoolgirl. Thankfully, we're not on a video call.

'I'm OK thank you. Did I ring at a bad time?'

'I'm sorry no, not at all,' I'm mortified that I can't talk properly to this man, I just turn into a gibbering wreck. I must pull myself together. 'I'm OK, it's just that I've been stuck in traffic for the last hour and a half as there's been an accident on the motorway. A tanker has tipped over and there's milk everywhere. It's pouring down and there's thunder and lightning on the horizon. So, I'm a little frazzled but I'm OK. I'm sorry about my tone, I didn't mean to sound so angry when I answered the

186

phone. Well, I did ... I mean it's so bloody frustrating. It was easier to drive to Cornwall from home than from Tenby. They should have a ferry boat or something to make the journey faster, I mean since when has there been so much sea between the two?' Amanda Markham get a bloody grip and take a breath!

Thankfully, Phil laughed good naturedly at my ramblings.

'It's OK, don't worry. I'm sorry to hear about the traffic, I agree, and Always.' He has answered each of my rambles quite succinctly and I find myself laughing along, my mood already lifting.

'Thank you for grounding me so nicely Mr Solicitor.' Oh God, and now I'm flirting. At least I think I am. What is wrong with me?

'Not a problem. I aim to please.' Is he flirting back? It's been so long I can't tell. I giggle, can you believe it? I'm 47 years old and I'm giggling. Blushing AND giggling AND using a bloody American accent y'all.

Chrissie would kill me if she heard me, but only after she had finished laughing at me.

'I was just ringing to see if you had received the divorce petition and also, erm to check that you were ... OK. I know it's not easy when the paperwork arrives. So, I erm just wanted to make sure you were ok.' He's as flustered as I am, which is a huge relief and I'm thrilled that he would even ask.

'Oh wow, thank you.' Act demure. 'Yes, I'm OK. I signed the paperwork and sent it back to you this morning, it's coming from Tenby, but hopefully you should get it tomorrow or the day after.' Well done, just keep it together. No soppy stuff. 'It just felt wrong to think that with a signature I'm ending a marriage, just a quick flick of the wrist and that's it.' Way to go Amanda, totally cool, not.

'Well, if it's any consolation it's taken a lot more than just a flick of the wrist.' He chuckles. 'But I know what you mean. It must be very hard to get over the shock of it all. That's the main reason I rang. I just wanted to make sure you were OK.'

'IT'S ABOUT BLOODY TIME!' I yell as the traffic has started to move.

'Oh right, err I'm sorry I haven't asked before, but I didn't think …'

'Oh God no, not you!' I am the worst person. He's flustering and I'm yelling. 'I'm so sorry. The traffic has started to move at last, and my excitement took over. I guess I shouldn't have cried over spilt milk ha ha.' Feeble joke I know but I told you I tend to ramble.

'No harm done. Well you … safe journey. I hope … a nice break and hopefully the ... will … good.' I can hardly hear him as the wind is shocking now and the heavens have opened, meaning the rain is absolutely bouncing down on the car.

'What? Phil? I can't hear you.' This is ridiculous. 'Hello?'

'I'll speak … whe … cornw … stay……………………………………………….'

'Sorry what? Hello? Phil are you there?' I try shouting but it's no use, he's gone. I've lost phone signal and, after a quick glance at my phone on the dashboard, I see not only that the bars have disappeared, but battery light is flashing too. Why can't things be simple? Why do I have to ramble when I talk to him? Why am I talking to myself? Do I need medical help?

Well, I can't do very much about my conversation with Phil now except analyse it to death, and as I'm not busy right now I'll get right on doing just that.

2 hours and 47 minutes later......

I've decided that I have imagined any spark or flirting between Phil and I and that he was just being friendly. Shame really, he's bloody gorgeous and a nice guy too. Rare quality in a man these days, or am I being a tad cynical?

Anyway, time to ponder later as I'm now outside the cottage and Terry is getting out of his Range Rover and bounding over, and he's thoughtfully brought a golfing umbrella as the rain is torrential.

'We thought you'd gotten lost?' says Terry, the rain dripping off the umbrella like he's stood under a shower. He helps me out of the car (Terry is old school, one of the rare gentlemen.) 'You alright then my love?'

I smile at his warm greeting as I grab my coat from the back seat. 'Better for being here Terry, that's for sure. Shame about the weather though!' He gives me a quick hug.

'Audrey's just on the phone taking a booking but she'll be with us in just a minute.' He leans forward and lowers his voice to a whisper, but on Terry it's more of a stage whisper so people in the next town can surely hear him. 'Before she comes over I need to talk to you in private so would it be OK if I pop round later?'   Ooh, this sounds intriguing.

'Sounds exciting. Yes, just call round when you can.' I stage whisper back.

He taps the side of his nose and winks just as Audrey gets out of the car. I'm sure she's spotted his little gesture, but he's too invested in his theatrics to notice.

'Amanda!' Audrey rushes over with her arms outstretched, greeting me like a long-lost relative and gives me a huge hug. Technically we've only really known each other for a week but I know that I've found lifelong friends in these two. Well, in all my Cornish pals really. They've all kept in touch either texting, phoning or emailing, and even John has been texting me, albeit to find out the answers to some quiz questions, but it still counts.

'You get yourself settled in and come over for a cup of tea. I even made some scones, and they're still warm.' She hands me the key to my home for the week. Hope the rain stops though.

'Clotted cream and jam?' I ask expectantly.

'Of course! We're not animals you know.' she laughs. 'Will you be OK coming round in the dark and in this weather?'

I tell her I'll be over in 20 minutes and that I'll be fine. Terry gives me another stage wink as he leaves. I'm sure that whatever he's hiding from Audrey, isn't being that well-hidden as he's not the best at the cloak and dagger stuff.

I wave them off and unpack my things, plugging my phone in as a priority. This time I've brought some provisions from home. Wine, bread, cheese. Obviously, everything that's bad for you, but what the hell, you only live once. So, naturally there's a little chocolate in there too.

The place looks no different, not that it should as it's only been a few months. But with it's beautiful white walls and blue door, surrounded only by the remnants of jasmine, it beckons me in to what I already call my home away from home. It's also nice to see it in the autumn, the rain battering on the windows may dampen the woodwork but not my good feeling.

I turn the lamps on and the amber glow that settles around the room makes me feel I never want to leave, that said there is a cream tea waiting for me, and it would be rude to turn down such hospitality. My tummy growls in acknowledgement.

My phone has come to life with just a little charge, so I fire off a couple of quick texts letting everyone know I'm here and while I'm doing this a text comes through from a number I don't recognise.

Hi! I seem to have lost you back there and guess that either a, there is no telephone signal where you are or b, your battery has died. Please direct all answers to this number as this is my personal phone. Phil

O.M.G. What is happening? First, he's flirting, now he's texting AND giving out his personal number. I haven't had butterflies in my stomach for years, but this man has them flapping around like mad. I'm aware that I have a stupid grin on my face. I send a quick reply.

Answers are a and b; a. I lost signal but b. my phone then died. I am here safe and sound and happy to be able to relax and think about nothing but the visit to my friends that awaits me right now. Thanks for texting.

Thanks for texting? Thanks for bloody texting? Well that's just great as you now look totally desperate for any male attention. He's going to think you're a desperate housewife or a desperate soon-to-be-ex-house-wife? Either that, or he's going to think you aren't interested. Enough! I can't think of this right now, so I leave my phone charging, lock up and head over for my cream tea. At least that won't be complicated.

The rain has lightened from a torrential downpour to a heavy drizzle, so I wrap up in my coat, scarf, gloves and boots, put my hood up, lock up and set off. It feels good to stretch my legs, even if it's only for the 5-minute walk to Audrey and Terry's home. But, after my long car journey, I feel slightly more refreshed and can't wait to update them on everything that's happened 'up north'. Plus, the cream tea is naturally a bonus.

Terry greets me at the door and again, goes into the worst acting I've seen since the BBC aired Eldorado.

'OH, HELLO MANDY! COME IN!' He bellows. Cue stage whisper ... 'It's Audrey's birthday in 3 weeks and I'm arranging a surprise party, but I could do with a …'

'Hello there, what kept you?' says Audrey as she comes into the lounge from the kitchen, wiping her hands on a tea towel. The smell from the kitchen is amazing. 'Let her in! Honestly Terry, fancy making her stand in the hallway, that's fellas for you.' She says, rolling her eyes. 'You get out of your wet coat and come on through and I'll put the kettle on. I've had to stand guard over the scones to stop Terry nicking any.' She laughs shaking her head. I'm not sure how she manages to say all that without much breath. I forgot what a lively character she was.

The cream tea catch up and furtive glances from Terry, as he's dying to fill me in on the surprise party, made the early evening a lovely one and I forgot my shocking journey.

'I think I'll head off home, well to the cottage now. It's been quite a long day and I'm done in.'

'I'll take you back!' Terry shouts from the kitchen, his radar ears on full alert.

'Blimey, he's not normally that helpful. Take him up on it quick love before he changes his mind!' Audrey laughs. I'm sure she knows something is going on, but I can't ask.

'Thanks Terry, that would be lovely and thank you for the delicious cream tea. I'll never be skinny at this rate.'

'You've lost weight since we saw you last. Hasn't she Terry? I said that to him the minute we left you at the cottage. I said, 'she's lost weight hasn't she Terry?' Didn't I?'

'Yes love, you did.'

'I said, 'I need to feed her up', didn't I Terry?'

'Yes love, you did.'

'Thank you,' I laugh. 'I'm not sure I need feeding up though.' These two make me smile all the time. Audrey with her bubbly nature and Terry with his calm agreeing one. I laugh and give her a hug and we agree to get together in the next couple of days. I wave as the car pulls away.

'Has she gone?' Terry asks. He must think she has the ears of a bat and can lip read in the dark. I tell him the coast is clear.

'Right. I'm putting on a surprise party for Audrey's birthday. I've drawn up a list of guests and there's only about twenty people going so I thought the private room at the local pub. What do you think? I'm worried it'll be too big though. To be honest love, I could do with a hand.'

'And you've thought of me? The newcomer?' I'm totally dumbfounded as to the trust this man has just put in me.

'Well yes, you seem to know everyone, and you look like you know how to plan a party.' I laugh at his confidence in me.

'Well, I guess that's settled.' I can't say no as he's looking at me so eagerly. 'I'm going into the village in the morning, so I can have a look around. Have you thought about food? A cake? Invitations? Decorations?' The blank look on his face tells me exactly how much thought has gone into those things.

'So, let me get this straight. You're having a surprise party, but you haven't invited anyone?'

'Yes.'

'Yes? Yes, you have or yes you haven't?'

'Yes, I have. I've rang everyone and they're all coming.'

'Do they know where the party is?'

'No.'

'Have you sorted the food? Cake? Decorations?'

'Erm, no, no and no, but I have bought a packet of balloons.' This makes me laugh my head off, but I stop abruptly at the look of helplessness on his face.

'OK, don't panic. So, 20 people and some balloons. I can work with that.' I squeeze his hand with reassurance. I only hope I don't let him down. 'I'll speak to you in the next couple of days with some ideas, but can you let me know who's coming?'

'It's basically the people you met when you were here. A couple more and some family. She only has one cousin and he said he's coming and then her aunty and uncle. So, with you and me and Audrey obviously, it's 19. Maybe your friend can come too?'

'OK, so when is her actual birthday and the party?'

'Saturday the 3rd December.'

'In 3 weeks? Blimey Terry, you've not left me much time. Don't panic, I can do this.' I say more for my benefit than Terry's.

With that we say goodnight and he leaves me to my home away from home. Well, I know I came down for a relaxing break, but I can think of nothing nicer than arranging a party for Audrey.

I've left the lights on at the cottage, so it still has that cosy feel and the central heating has left it nice and warm for me. I get out of my winter outerwear and head upstairs for a quick shower.

Twenty minutes later I'm snug in my pyjamas with a cup of tea and my mobile phone which is bursting with messages from the kids, Chrissie, mum and (tingle) Phil. I answer everyone's messages before I go to Phil's (plural!).

Hope you have a good evening. I'll send your papers to courts as soon as I receive them and let you know the outcome. Speak to you soon. Phil

Oh, that was anticlimactic. I'm surprised at the disappointment I feel, he was obviously just being friendly after all. I check the next message.

By the way, I meant to say it was lovely to see you out the other week. You looked lovely. I'm sorry I had to go so quickly.

I'm smiling, no I'm grinning. Well, I can say for sure that this comes under the 'friendly' category, but romantic friendly and not platonic friendly and can I stop saying the word friendly?

I had a lovely time thanks. OK, re divorce.

What do I put to the second message?

Thank you. It was great to see you and you looked good too. I knew you'd look great out of your work clothes.

What? Oh God, don't send that. Delete it. BLOODY DELETE! Noooo! Who puts the send button right on top of the delete button? I've sent it and now I can't un-send it. I've gone from slightly flirty to practically telling him I'll make him eggs in the morning. I dread to think what he's going to put.

Hahaha thank you

Hmm, I'm glad he has a sense of humour.

Not quite what I meant but you're welcome. I'm going to drown myself in the Atlantic Ocean now.

Please don't do that. You haven't paid your bill yet!

LOL

I'll see you when you get back.

Ok. See you soon

I need to talk to Chrissie, NOW.

'OK, tell me word for word what he wrote and what you said.' I put her on speaker and go to my text messages. Her raucous laughter rings around the cottage at my suggestive reply regarding his clothes, or potential lack of. 'Oh Mand, you are hilarious.'

'What do I do now? I replied with a LOL. LOL! Like I'm a bloody teenager. I almost sent him a smiley face but stopped myself. He's going to think I'm an idiot.'

'No, he isn't. He obviously likes you. I can tell you now that he's never text me and I'm his best client. Now love, you do nothing. You said the last bit and now it's his turn. Like a game of chess, he might be a while taking his turn, but you can't butt in and have your go yet. There's a strategy, and you have to be patient.'

'Right, patient, OK I can do that. Is this how it is now? Strategic thinking? What happened to spontaneity?' It's been so long since I've dated anyone, I don't want to mess it up and I know Chrissie will tell me exactly how it is. 'Should I even be thinking about this now? I'm not even divorced yet!'

'You will be divorced in a matter of weeks and you're not dead love, just possibly dating.' She laughs at my overreaction. 'Just relax and let what may happen, happen.'

'You're right,' I knew that she would know what to do. 'In the meantime, are you free on Saturday 3 December?'

I tell her all about Terry's theatrics and about the fact that I agreed to help him with this party. Although, I'm still not sure why he's asked me when there are other people in the village who would be far better sourced for this project. Chrissie said she'll be there but probably with Simon, which is fine. The more the merrier.

We say goodnight, and I promise to let her know if I hear anything else from Phil. I take a drink up to bed and lie there re-reading the text messages until I fall asleep smiling.

The following day starts frosty with a clear blue sky and a gorgeous view out over the ocean. All signs of last night's storm are gone if you discount the branches and leaves dotted around the garden. It makes me smile just to see out to the beach and beyond. It really would be amazing to live here, to wake up to this every day. I don't think I would ever tire of it even though we're in November and it's freezing out there.

I get up and put the kettle on and grab my pad where I have written down the things I need to do.

<u>Surprise party to do list:</u>

1. Find venue
2. Decorations
3. Cake
4. Food
5. Guests
6. Find B&B

So, not too much to sort out in three weeks then. After a quick breakfast and a slow shower, I walk into the town and my first stop is John, my wonderful butcher.

'Well, hello there my love!' He comes over to give me a hug but thinks better of it when he looks down at his ever present, bloodied apron and pats my shoulder instead. 'It's so good to see you back. Quiz night Wednesday?'

'Hi John, of course. I wouldn't miss it, in fact I'm quite excited. I hope those Witty Warriors have been behaving themselves?'

'Well, there was a bit of an issue the other week when they accused me of texting you a question. I mean, can you believe the cheek of them?' He puffs out his chest and shakes his head.

'But John, you were texting me.' I laugh.

'Aye, that I was, but they weren't to know that, now were they?' His sly smile and waggling eyebrows make me laugh again.

I tell him about Audrey's surprise party and he says he'll help wherever he can. I buy some provisions from him and head off to visit my other new friends.

Everyone greets me like I'm their best friend and it makes me feel wonderful. They have all agreed to help with food and I have agreed to go to the next Salsa class as Julio was missing me. Mary has said that she'll do the cake and she knows Audrey from school and they're the same age which means she will be 60. I can't believe it to be honest. The vivaciousness that comes off her in waves knocks years off her. I must take a few pointers from her.

One thing I've realised, just from staying here last time and again now, I find myself saying 'yes' to everything. Yes, to Salsa. Yes, to quiz night. Yes, to Karaoke. Yes, to arranging a party for Audrey (although I might live to regret that decision).

I don't know when I stopped saying yes to things and became Mundane Mandy, but I like the new me. I'm happy. Maybe it's just this place, I don't know, but there's a new me here and I like the uncertainty of my future. I can do anything I want to. Maybe I'll try a parachute jump or learn to surf. Then again, better walk before I can run eh?

Back to the issue of the venue. I can check out the church hall, but it will probably be a bit big for just twenty people. I'm sure that Terry must have missed some people off his list. I mean I've only been here twice and I know half that many people already and Audrey has lived here all her life. I'll get a copy of the list from him and speak to the others at quiz night.

I pop into the Dog and Duck for a bite of lunch and to check out the function room they let out for parties. It's not bad actually. I mean it needs a spruce up and a bit of birthday/Christmas cheer, but it will be perfect.

Lunch was butternut squash and sweet potato soup with crusty bread. It was delicious, and I tell the landlord Gary just that.

'Thank you, we've got ourselves a new chef all the way from some swanky restaurant in London. Said he'd had enough of the fast pace and wanted a change so he packed up and came here. Lucky us, that's what I say. He's had us eating all kinds of weird stuff and not just the soup!' He shakes his head laughing as he heads off to serve someone at the bar.

I'm not sure the soup would come under the 'weird' category but, pardoning the pun, he's given me food for thought. This guy just packed up his life in London and moved here for a change of scenery and a calmer life? Maybe he just decided to start saying yes to things too. Well done him! Could I do it? Could I leave everything and everybody I know and start all over again down here? I know I have to pack up everything anyway, but I need to speak to the kids and see what they think, and what about Chrissie? My job? And I know nothing has happened yet, but what about Phil?

Ping. A text message from Phil. (Does he have some sixth sense?) My stomach butterflies are back.

Hi, just letting you know that I have your paperwork back and I will send it all off to the courts in the next couple of days. I'll keep you updated. Hope you're having a good time. P

Act cool Amanda. No commenting on his attire or supposed nakedness.

Hi, thanks for telling me. It's gorgeous here. Just had lunch and off for a walk now. The sun is shining and not a cloud in the sky, it's still freezing but lovely. M x

Aaarrggghhh, I put a kiss! A bloody kiss! What is wrong with me? I know I do it with everyone and I automatically did it with him. But a sodding kiss! What can I do about it now?

'You calm the hell down for one thing and hello to you too.' Chrissie laughs as I tell her my disaster. 'Is that it? A little x at the end of a text isn't the end of the world you know. I put them on everyone's. I even put one on the end of a message to my dentist once.'

'The one you slept with doesn't count.' I reply. 'Seriously, am I being too forward?'

'Fuck me woman be realistic, you've not offered to have sex with the man, have you?'

'No, of course not!'

'So, it's fine. It's friendly, flirtatious and a little fun too, which does no harm. When was the last time you were flirted with anyone?'

'I think when Jennifer Rush was number one in the charts.' She laughs but I'm just blushing and shaking my head.

'Give over, you really need to relax and be yourself. It's just an x. At least you didn't go the full hog and put hearts and kissy emoji's.' I know she's laughing at me, but she has calmed me down.

Ping.

'Oh, hang on I've just received another text, I'll put you on speaker phone and check.'

'I shall wait with baited breath.' She teases.

'Oh, sod off.' I laugh. The text is from Phil.

I love it down there. Have a great time and relax. See you when you get back. P x

'Oh my God! He's put a kiss too!' I hear myself and am ashamed at my immaturity but secretly thrilled as well. I thought I'd hid my joy but from the looks and smiles I'm getting from the other customers in the pub, it wasn't so secret after all.

'Right, you saddo. Are you OK now? Can I get back to work and people who have real problems?' She's still laughing at me as she hangs up and I'm still grinning like the Cheshire Cat.

I pay the bill for my lunch and head out, ignoring the look of amusement on Gary's face.

I'm in no rush to get back, so I just take a walk around the town. I buy some more pencils from the art and craft shop and look at their Christmas and Birthday decorations which sparks an idea about the party. I need to have a think about it more, but I believe I have an idea forming.

I stop outside the estate agents, just to pass the time of course. The prices are high that's for sure but there are some more reasonable ones if I, I mean anyone, wants to move here.

I walk back along the beach road and take some photos with the thought that I could possibly paint them when I get home. The sun is low at this time of year and it glistens off the sea making it shimmer with diamonds.

I keep thinking about the texts from Phil and am still smiling about the kiss on the end of his P, ahem, you know what I mean. It's just nice to remember that I'm a woman as well as a mum and soon to be ex-wife.

Back at the cottage I cosy up with my book, a brew and a bit of home-made fudge from the sweet shop in the village. Diet be damned, I'm on holiday!

Chapter 21

'Is this it?' I look at the flimsy scrap of paper that Terry has given me, which is complete with coffee ring.

'Aye. Why what's wrong with it?' He looks at me with worry and confusion.

I smile and put the kettle on as I think this is a tea and biscuit moment (not that I need an excuse really).

'It's just that there aren't many people on it. Didn't you both grow up here?' I ask, hoping he can give me something to work with.

'Yes, we did,' he looks proud of the fact. 'We went to the same infants, junior and secondary school. You should have seen her. She used to have the most ridiculous pigtails. Came right out of the top of her head they did!' Terry laughs at the memory, but you can see the absolute love written on his face. I laugh along and feel a jolt of emotion. This man would never leave his beloved wife for another woman, no matter how young and flexible she is.

'Don't worry, it's a start. What about photographs of Audrey? It would be nice if we could decorate the room with a few pictures of her life as a child and your life together.' His face falls.

'A few years ago, we had a fire. Faulty wiring on the tumble drier in the garage they said. We lost everything.' He looks crestfallen.

'Oh Terry, that's awful! Neither one of you were hurt, were you?'

'No, we just lost all our memories.' He sighs, but then smiles and taps his head. 'I still have them all up here though.'

'You are an amazing man Terry Booth.' I give his arm a squeeze and I smile at the blush that spreads over his cheeks. 'Let's have a brew and see what we can come up with together.'

I get my pad out of my bag and look at his list again, which doesn't take very long.

His grand guest list is as follows:

PARTY
Me and Audrey
John + 1
Mary + 1
Tina + Ste
Kay + Darren
Tony + 1
Brian + Marie

Amanda and her friend Christine
1 cousin
Aunty Elsie and Uncle Roy

'I'm just thinking that there must be more people who would want to celebrate Audrey's 60th with her. What about old school friends?'

'Erm, well, I don't know.' He scratches his head as he thinks. 'I guess there are more people, but I just can't remember their names.' His puppy dog look is more than I can bear.

'Terry, you've only known me for a total of 9 days. How on earth do you know if I'll get it right?' I'm flabbergasted at the trust this man has put in me, but if he's happy then who am I to judge?

'You're a good person and a thoughtful one. You've picked up on everyone's personalities and it's like you've watered them and they've all blossomed into a brighter version of themselves.'

Bloody hell, this is the most Terry has said to me in the whole time I've known him, who knew he could be so deep. (I know it's only 9 days but still.)

'Wow, thank you. I didn't know you thought that.' I puff up with pride.

'Well, to be honest they're Audrey's words not mine.' Admits Terry, and I laugh. His candour is refreshing so I get my party planning head on.

'OK, do you mind if I have a word in the village with a few people I've met and see if they can come up with any ideas?'

'No, no not at all. That's smashing love. I knew you wouldn't let me down.' He's patting my arm now and has chirped up no end. He's finished his cup of tea and is even on his fourth chocolate digestive. I think I'm onto his game now, albeit a little late. Cheeky beggar.

'Any chance of a refill my love?'

I spend the evening with a long soak in the bath, a catch up with the kids and a lovely romcom about a woman who owns her mums book store but must sell because this horrible guy opens a huge one and puts her out of business. Well it sounds rubbish explained like that, but it was lovely.

One thing I told the kids was that I had been asked to arrange Audrey's party and it had planted a seed in my head. I have decided that I want to have a Christmas party at the house and it will be lovely to have everyone together. To be honest it will help me too as it's the first Christmas I'll be on my own and I think the last one we'll have at the house too. They've all agreed and I'm so excited. Having my family and the little one's around on Christmas morning, waking up to their presents is just the tonic I need.

I do have to think about things with Andy and Zooey. I'm done being angry, for now anyway, at least unless he does something stupid which, given his track record, could be any day really. We do need to work out a way that we can communicate without shouting, or solicitors mediating. What if one of the kids had a party and wanted to invite us both? I mean, Billy isn't married and what if he finds the right person? Or, if Ellie and Jackie decide to marry. It would be awful for them, and us too if there was a bad atmosphere. I need to think about this more, but the anger has gone so at least that's a start. I head off to bed with a more positive mind. Time to start afresh.

I wake up the following morning, always a good thing, fresh and full of optimism for the day ahead. I'm going to see Mary and ask if there is anyone she thinks we should invite to the surprise birthday bash and to discuss the cake with her. I also think that the pub is a great venue and I need to speak to Gary to see if he will decorate it with a Christmas theme and what food they could put on.

I'll OK all this with Terry next time I see him but at least I have a start.

By 10.00am I'm sat in Mary's bakery, with the most amazing smells all around me. Bread, cakes, cinnamon … mmm I've drifted off into carb heaven.

'Sorry Mary, did you say something? It's just that there are too many lovely smells in here for me to concentrate. I'm definitely going to buy some of those cinnamon rolls before I leave.'

'It's fine Pet,' she chuckles. 'I'm glad you like them. Now, about Audrey, I know there are about a dozen or so of us left around here that Mary knows. Terry's such a lamb but he's a typical man, he can't see what's under his nose.'

A customer walks in and Mary goes off to serve them while I sit in my bakery bliss and my thoughts drift to Phil. I know I will have to leave speaking to him until I get home, but I must admit I'm really looking forward to it. A few months ago, I wouldn't believe anyone if they said I'd be having lewd thoughts about another man. Oh, didn't I mention they were lewd? They were very, very lewd indeed.

'What or who's got you smiling like the cat who got the cream?' I hadn't realised that the customer had left, and Mary was looking at me, smiling.

'Oh nothing, just thinking about the party that's all.' I know I'm blushing, but I can put it down to a hot flush if she asks. 'So, erm a dozen people you say. Is that with or without partners?'

'I'd say about 18 in total as some are widowed but, if you say they can bring someone then you're looking at 24. Audrey was such a funny girl, I don't mean odd, but she was always making everyone laugh and she was a stunner that's for sure. There was many a sad boy when Terry swooped in and took her for himself. They've only had eyes for each other ever since. It was such a shame they couldn't have children. They would have made wonderful parents.'

'I did wonder but you don't like to ask; for some people it's a life choice.' I deal with this a lot at work. Couples going through hell month after month and then try IVF treatment, but that doesn't work either. 'It's so sad when people who should be parents can't, and then people who shouldn't seem to pop them out for fun.'

'Oh, don't get me started on that. There's a woman in the village that has had three children taken into care and is now pregnant again! It's a crying shame for those little kiddies.'

'I know what you mean. I have a few couples who come to see me at work and it's heart-breaking to hear them blame themselves.'

Another customer pops in and Mary gives her full attention to them and even takes the time to ask about their ill father. Top marks for customer service.

'Bye Mandy.' The customer smiles and waves as she's leaving.

'Oh, erm bye.' I can't believe how lovely this town is. How does she know me? Mary just carries on talking to me as though there had been no break in conversation. 'Did Terry tell you his birthday is only a couple of weeks later?'

'No, the dark horse didn't. What if we make it a surprise party for them both, even though one of them knows about it and I think the other suspects?'

'Ooh, this is so exciting. A surprise, surprise party! I'll put the kettle on while you grab us a couple of cinnamon rolls and I'll see if I can think of anyone Terry might like there too.'

We spend the rest of the morning adding people to the list and serving customers. Mary even has some school photos so is going to dig them out, so I can enlarge them and display them in the room. By the time we're done, I have quite the feat in front of me. It looks like it's going to be one heck of a party.

Chapter 22

The next couple of days are spent gathering information for the party and secretly including Terry in the surprise. I've still had time for walking doing some sketches on the beach, but it has been so cold that my fingers could only hold the pencil for so long before they went numb. I had another great night at the Salsa class and Julio was so thrilled to see me that he insisted on dancing with me the whole time, much to everyone's amusement.

Mary has kindly agreed to do the cake to suit both Audrey and Terry and is going to invite all their old school pals so that's another couple of things off the list. As for family, Terry is a bit like Audrey and they are quite thin on the ground. There was an uncle that moved to

Australia but that was it, so I'm sticking with friends instead.

I went back to look at the room at the pub and Gary let me check out his Christmas decorations. He is sworn to secrecy and has promised a DJ and his new chef, Dean is going to do the buffet. Everyone I have spoken to about the party, thinks the world of the birthday pair and are all more than happy to help (even to the point that they either insist on doing it free of charge or at the most, cost price). So, all that's left for me to do is sort out a large banner to wish them both happy birthday, get some photographs enlarged (which Mary will give me before I go home), and arrange additional decorations for the room. I'm so excited and happy to be able to give something back to these wonderful people.

I feel quite giddy with it all to be honest. Other than when the children were younger, I haven't hosted or planned any parties for years. To be honest, it's not been something I've thought about. You just get used to plodding along and not taking life by the horns (or whatever bit of life you grab hold of) and living life to the max. It's so easy to fall into a rut in life and I'm as guilty as the next person, but down here I feel different. I feel confident, funny even and surprisingly well liked.

I have been welcomed into this little community without any judgement and I feel humbled by their acceptance. I know when I go home the house will need to be put on the market and deep down I think the kids know it too, but what then? I could buy a new place where I live now, and I would be comfortable, but would I be happy? The area is nice, but everyone there knows me as

Andy's wife and the kids mum (regardless of their ages).
Here I'm Mandy and I can be myself or rather my old,
new and improved self. Mandy 2.0.

I do have a little confession. I have been looking at
top properties online and in the estate agent's windows,
but nothing has jumped out at me. Obviously, I still need
to think about my job and the career I've built up even
though, after the divorce is finalised and the house is sold
I will be financially comfortable, but I can't imagine not
working. What would I do with myself? Much as I love
it here and the break is doing me so much good, for my
sanity alone, I really to work. I have tossed around the
idea of setting up my own business. Maybe have a
separate place built that would either be attached to the
house or at the bottom of the garden. My very own clinic.
Could I do it? Do they need such a service? Blimey,
wouldn't that shock everyone? I make a separate note to
check out the local doctor's surgery's and hospices and
ask them what they have on offer.

My head is a muddle of thoughts right now and I really
do need to talk to my family and Chrissie before I make
any life altering decisions, so I'll pop any thought of
moving to a new house on the back burner for now and
focus on the party. So, it's back to the list.

The Surprise/Surprise Party

1. Find venue - done
2. Decorations -   Christmas and 60's theme -
    pub/me
3. Cake - Mary - done

4. Food - Chef at pub - done
5. Guests - Mary again - done
6. Book B&B

Well, that was easy. All I need to do is discuss food options with the new chef, Dean and that's planned for tomorrow, which means that today I have a free day. As I obviously can't book the cottage again for the party, I'm going to look for a B&B for me, Chrissie and Simon. Obviously, it can't be anything too local as we run the risk of bumping into the birthday girl and boy. A trip out of town is needed.

The roads leading out of Port Isaac are narrow and dotted with an eclectic mix of bungalows, houses and cottages, old and new. Even in this season, where there's frost on the hawthorn bushes, and leafless trees, it's starkness still stunning.

It's beautiful where I live now, with its lush green countryside and little villages, but the thing that gives Cornwall the edge, for me at least, are the sudden glimpses of ocean through the trees. That's what brings all the childhood memories back, that's what I want each day. It's something I'm going to investigate seriously in the new year. I'm getting butterflies just thinking about it.

About 10 minutes out of town I find a gorgeous Bed and Breakfast. It looks like an old farmhouse and it's painted mint green with white windows and front door. Lucky for me the owner, Marjorie, tells me she has 2 rooms for the weekend of the party, so that's another thing to tick off my list.

This area is so pretty with its narrow lanes with high hedges, but I'll be stuck if any cars come my way though. Now and again I see my favourite views of the sea with occasional glimpses of the waves crashing on the rocks. It's quite a blustery day and the ground is covered in a mix of russets, orange and brown leaves, all topped with a sprinkling of frost.

As I have nothing else to do today, I take the opportunity to go for a walk. I park the car, and with my pad and pencils now having a permanent place in my bag, I set off in search of something interesting to draw. The town has a small church, a pub, a convenience store and a gift shop/cafe. Everything you need in a 500m radius.

I walk through the village (which takes all of 5 minutes) and admire the thatched cottages and neat gardens. Out the other side of this busy metropolis there are even less houses, but the views are breath-taking. Rolling green hills dotted with dry stone walls from centuries ago that have withstood the varied climate of the west coast. It makes you wonder whether the modern houses and garden walls of today will still be standing in another 200 years. I think not.

Just off the 'main road', still only wide enough for a tractor at most there is an even smaller lane. Slightly overgrown from lack of use, I decide to explore. This is the joy of walking on your own. You have no set agenda, no one to worry about whether they want to go down this road or that, no one glancing at their watch to hurry you on. As you gather, I'm really enjoying this new way of life. For the first time in a long time, I feel free.

Two hundred yards down the lane I come across a rather rundown house. It's double fronted with a window either side of the front door and two upstairs windows. Surprisingly there is a For Sale sign in the garden, although there definitely wasn't one on the main road. Even more surprising is the smoke coming from the chimney. From this view it looks like it could have 3 bedrooms but obviously I'm only guessing. What I can see, is a large garden.

Granted this time of year, it's not at its best but it wraps around the whole house and I can see established bushes and borders with heathers and hebe's. There's also a detached garage with half the roof missing and an overgrown driveway to this narrow lane that I'm standing on.

'Hello. You see enough?' I hadn't realised the front door had opened, but there was an elderly lady on the doorstep wiping her hands on her apron.

'Oh, hello. I'm so sorry I was staring at your house, I'm not usually that nosy. Well I probably am, but I've never been caught before.' I laugh and thankfully so does she.

'Well, I like your honesty. You must be freezing standing out there. Would you like a cup of tea?' She wipes her hands on her tea towel and stands with her arms folded over her chest. .I don't get many visitors up here.'

Now I know we are taught not to accept drinks from strangers and to never, ever go into their house, but I think I could take her in an arm wrestle, so I accept her kind offer and look forward to thawing my feet in front of her fire.

'I see your house is for sale.'

'It is. Are you looking for one?' She looks at me with raised eyebrows as I walk over her threshold and into her wonderfully cluttered kitchen.

'I'm not sure actually.' I answer as best as I can.

'Well, I think a person should know if they are or are not.' She laughs, reminding me of Yoda ('The Force' is strong in this one). 'Have a seat by the fire and warm yourself.'

It seems that no one has viewed the house for months now and I tell her that there is no 'For Sale' sign on the main road and had I not wandered up here I would never have found it.

'Well, the right person will come along when they're ready.' She answers rather cryptically.

'Would you like me to ring the estate agent?' I pull my phone out of my pocket.

'Oh no dear,' she shakes her head. 'I'm in no rush. Would you like to stay for some soup? I've made enough.'

'That would be lovely, thank you.' Well, it would be rude to turn her down and it does smell delicious.

The tomato soup tasted delicious and is served with homemade bread, followed by more tea and homemade biscuits and we spend the next couple of hours chatting about life, children, divorce, Australian physiotherapists and new opportunities.

Her name is Harriet and she is delightful, insightful, and at 85 is the feistiest octogenarian I have ever met. Understandably, the house is becoming harder for her to manage as repairs are so expensive and she has her eye on one of the 'Warden controlled' bungalows in the local town. In the short time I've known her, I already feel like I've made yet another friend and I hope she feels the same.

Obviously, I'm dying to have a nosy around but it's not something I can bring up, so I just take in the room where we have sat for the last few hours. It has curtains instead of cupboard doors on the base units and an original Belfast sink. On the wall not housed with units, there is a welsh dresser full of dishes, ornamental cats, books and letters, giving the room a lovely, lived in and very, very homely feel.

There are 2 comfy threadbare armchairs in front of the open fire and an Aga giving off heat on the other side of the room. I hope I'm not being too obvious with my surreptitious glances around, I do like to think that I can be discreet.

'Would you like to see the rest of the house?' she laughs. 'I'm sure by now you could probably tell me what's in this room more than I can.' She cackles at me, her eyes twinkling with mischief. At least I have the grace to blush.

'I'm sorry, it's just that your home is amazing.'

'It's been called cluttered, disorganised and old before, but then again so have I!' She winks. 'But, amazing? Now, that's a first. Come on.' I laugh along as she leads the way to the other rooms.

The house really is lovely and doesn't disappoint as we go from room to room, confirming what I already thought regarding the original features you would expect from an old farmhouse. Beams, Aga, open fires and more, are all intact. There are cast iron fireplaces in all the bedrooms, of which there are three in total and a cast iron roll top bath in the bathroom. Don't get me wrong, I can see that the features have been retained more out of circumstance than anything else, but I love it.

'How long has it been for sale?' I ask, trying to show politeness and not giving away the fact that the butterflies in my stomach are dancing around. Could I do it? Could I up sticks and start life again, here? I keep my face neutral as I look at her.

'Why? Are you interested?' Her eyes twinkle with mischief as she waggles here eyebrows at me.

'I can get nothing past you, can I? Either I'm rubbish at hiding what I'm thinking, or you've got a gift at reading people.'

'You're rubbish at hiding what you're thinking,' she laughs. 'And I have a gift. I've known you for a few hours and I can see you wear your heart on your sleeve. Don't get me wrong, that's not a bad thing, it just shows that you care.'

I'm speechless (which doesn't happen often). This beautiful lady, who has known me for such a short time, has summed me up in nutshell. I left Harriet with a promise to call again before I go home, and I have the estate agents details safely stored in my phone. Just in case.

The rest of the week flies by with Quiz night, Karaoke and another visit to see Harriet. It was so hard making sure I didn't slip up and tell Audrey that I would see her in a couple of weeks.

'Well, you have a safe drive home now.' Audrey has come to say goodbye with Terry. Her eyes are full of tears.

'Hey, what's the matter?' I put my arm around her small frame and can smell her trademark fragrance of hairspray and Chanel Number 5.

'Oh, don't mind me love. I'm just a beggar.' She wipes her eyes and gives her nose a wipe. 'It's just that when you're here, it feels right and we're not going to see you for ages now. You will come back, won't you?'

'Try and keep me away.' I smile at them both. 'Honestly, being here has been the tonic I needed and to feel so comfortable in a place I've basically spent two week in, is amazing. I can't thank you all enough.' Now I have tears in my eyes. All we need now is for Terry to start and I'll never be able to leave.

'Oh, wait. I forgot something.' Audrey rushes off to the car, leaving Terry and me alone.

'So, are you ok with everything we've planned?' I ask him in a hushed tone.

'Aye you've done us proud my love, and thanks again. I couldn't have done this without you.' We stop talking as Audrey comes back with a present in her hands.

'It's just a little something for Christmas.'

'You didn't have to do that.' I'm overcome with emotion as I pull her into a hug.

'Oh, don't be daft. It's just a little something, so you don't forget us.' Audrey sniffs and wipes her eyes.

'As if!'

We have one final embrace before I get in the car and set off with a wave. I watch them waving back until I turn the corner where I need to pull the car over, tears are blocking my vision as I know I'm going to miss, not only them, but everyone else too. I acknowledge the fact that I don't want to leave but remind myself that I can come back anytime and will in fact be here in a couple of weeks. I calm down, wipe my eyes, pop a chocolate éclair sweet into my mouth, crank the music up and set off again.

Chapter 23

It was a long drive back home and dark and dreary for most of the way, a bit like how I was feeling. I'd left everyone with their tasks for the party and I'm most excited about the cake, as from what Mary has told me it is going to be amazing. She is making a 3-tier cake, each layer a different flavour; chocolate, lemon and Victoria sponge. All filled and covered buttercream with miniature photo frames all around each layer showing Audrey and Terry growing up.

Lucky for us, Mary has found her old school pictures and some photographs from their wedding and by chance, some more recent one's from other social events, so there are photo's showing their whole lives. (The positives of growing up in a small town.)

Dean is on board with the food for the buffet which is going to be typical 1960's party food; Vol au vents, cheese straws, quiche Lorraine, cocktail sausages and scotch eggs to name but a few. I just need to sort the birthday banner out and get the photographs that Mary has given me enlarged. Hopefully it will be a night to remember and I'm already buzzing with excitement.

Since coming home I have had a couple of text messages from Phil (each ending with a P x). He asks how I am and has said that it would be nice to get coffee some time, but they are mainly just to tell me that the divorce papers are now with the courts and he's waiting for the judge to pronounce the Decree Nisi. 6 weeks and one day on and I will be a divorcee. Unfortunately, this falls a few days before Christmas and I really don't want it to spoil our celebrations.

I'm not angry with Andy anymore but I am sad and selfishly I hope he is too. I know he's moved on and will be moving away to the other side of the world soon, but we had a whole life together, grew up together and granted, if I'm being honest with myself, we had grown apart together. Now I just need to work out where I'm going. Will my life be in Cheshire with Chrissie? Or, will it be further south? I think I already know the answer but I'm not quite ready to say it aloud.

I've been back at work for a couple of days and am finding it very hard to connect with my life. I don't think that my clients can tell, at least I hope not, but I still feel that I'm letting them down.

Chrissie is 'loved up' with Simon, so I've not seen much of her, except for at work, but I'm so happy for her, and for Simon too; Chrissie is a wonderful woman and I can see she's as besotted with him as he is with her.

I am excited about Christmas though, and the thought that I'll have all my family around me. I've started shopping for gifts and ordered my food in advance of the festivities. I do like to be organised and it's another thing to tick off one of my ever-present lists.

Today, I've had a lovely lunch at Ellie and Jackie's. Their home is a two bedroomed apartment in the centre of Manchester, close to their favourite bars and nightclubs. We only live around an hour away from each other, but I really don't see enough of them. I'll see even less if I move to Cornwall.

'Ellie, I'm so full, I think you're going to have to roll me to the car.' I groan. 'The pavlova finished me off, but I'm never one to pass up a pudding.'

We all laugh and then a look passes between the two of them.

'Mum, we have some news.' Ellie blushes and nods to Jackie.

'Mrs H, I hope we have your permission, but I've asked Ellie to marry me and she said yes!' I look at Ellie who has the biggest grin on her face. She waggles her hand at me, flashing a beautiful solitaire diamond ring, which I'm certain wasn't there before as I'm sure I would have noticed.

My eyes instantly fill up as I go around the table and pull my darling Ellie into a hug.

'Sweetheart, I couldn't be happier.' I say, turning to Jackie.

'Jackie, you have made not only my Ellie happy, but me too. I couldn't be prouder to call you my daughter-in-law.' We have a great big group hug as they fill me in on the details of the proposal and wedding plans.

'Jackie had planned a weekend away to London.'

'I was taking her to her favourite restaurant there.'

'Yes, but I took ill with food poisoning, so Jackie had to cancel it.' She gave Jackie's hand a squeeze.

'I had it all planned, Mrs H.' Jackie continued. 'It was a right swanky place, you've

 got to book it a month in advance. I was going to order a bottle of champagne when we got there, and then when I felt the time was right, I was going to pop the question.'

I watched them tell the rest of the tale perfectly in sync, with each of them picking up where the other left off. It was like watching a tennis match and I couldn't help but smile at the pair of them. Apparently, Ellie was so distraught at ruining a lovely weekend away (even though she didn't know about the restaurant) that Jackie decided to propose there and then, with a sick bucket as a witness.

'I'm still owed a weekend in London though!' said Jackie, as she playfully nudged Ellie.

'Where was your ring?' I asked my beaming daughter. 'It wasn't on your finger when I arrived, was it?' I couldn't believe I would have missed it.

'God no!' Ellie laughed. 'I had the ring in my front pocket, otherwise I knew you'd see it as soon as you got here,' Ellie laughs. 'Nothing gets past you mum.'

They plan to get married next year and are both open minded about where to have the ceremony. Now that they've told me, Ellie can't wait to ring her brother and sister and then her dad. We talked about him, and what would happen at the wedding and Ellie had a little cry. I assured her that we would be fine and there would be no nasty outbursts. It was their special day and we were mature enough to act with dignity.

The afternoon ends on the high of engagement rings and wedding plans. I asked the happy couple if they would both be wearing suits or dresses, but Jackie said she would feel more comfortable in a suit and Ellie wants a dress. I can't wait to help them plan for it, and with her dad and I funding it, the day was destined to be a grand one.

The roads weren't too busy on my journey home which I was glad about as my head is full of so much now that I can't think straight. Wedding, divorce, selling my home and where to live, Christmas, kids, Chrissie and then, Phil.

I know that there is something there with him but I'm not sure what's going to happen. Do I pursue it, knowing that I'm thinking of moving away? Would that be fair? Am I running before I can walk? Should I really keep talking to myself?

To save my head from imploding I turn to my number one guy Mr Rogers, and the two of us, well 403 if you count Lucille and her 400 hundred children, sing our hearts out. My phone, which was in the holder on my dash, pinged a few times during the drive but all that I could see when I glanced at the screen was a number I didn't recognise. They will have to wait until I get home.

Rudely I feel, during a particularly good rendition of 'The Gambler', my phone rings and it's the same number as the texts, so it's obviously someone desperate to talk to me. I press answer on my handsfree and say hello.

'Hello Amanda.'

It's a voice I haven't heard in over six months. I can't speak, I am cold with shock and my heart is pounding so hard I can hear it. It's Andy. I'm not ready for this, I'm not prepared. I hang up, I can't do this right now. I'm driving on a bloody motorway in the bloody rain and he picks now to ring! I know I'm being irrational, as he doesn't know where I am, but I don't care. How dare he? How dare he ring and calmly say 'hello Amanda' like it's nothing. Like he's just ringing to say he'll be late for dinner. I'm shaking with a rage that I didn't know I had. I guess I am still angry and had just bottled it up. You would think I ought to have realised that being a counsellor, but it's a lot easier to see these things in others rather than in ourselves.

The phone rings again and I see it's Andy again. I press decline. The services are just over a mile away and after declining four more calls, I pull into the service station and turn my phone off. My hands are shaking so bad that I struggle to press the off button. I get myself a cup of tea and some chocolate (old habits and all that) and I sit there staring at my now silent phone, unsure of what to do. I've gone from being happy and excited, to fractured in two words. *Hello Amanda.*

I knew this man for 33 years, but the shock of hearing his voice has knocked me sideways. I was on cloud 9 for my Ellie, and now I'm sub-zero. *Hello Amanda.*

I need Chrissie. We've been friends for so long that I know her number off by heart, so I go to the payphone and ring her. I worry she won't answer as this isn't a number she knows but thankfully she does.

'If you're asking about PPI, bank charges or an accident I haven't had you can f…'

'Chrissie, it's me.' Embarrassingly I start to cry, in public. People are walking past and trying not to look but failing miserably.

'Mand? What's happened? Where are you?'

'Andy rang.'

'Fuck!'

'Oh Chrissie.' I sob.

'What did he say? I hope you gave him what for? And by the way, where the hell are you ringing from?'

'He said, 'Hello Amanda' and I hung up.' Tears are pouring down my face. 'I'm at a service station just near my exit. I'll be home in 20 minutes. I couldn't drive. I've switched my phone off in case he rings again.' I say all this through my sobs.

'Right, OK. You've had a shock but you're OK. Have you got a cup of tea and some chocolate?' The woman knows me so well. 'Good, have those, get in the car and put that crap music on that you like and get home. We'll sort the rest out when you get here.'

We agree to meet at mine and it's the longest 20-minute drive I've ever taken. With the winter evenings starting earlier it's dark by the time I get home. I pull into the driveway and am so grateful that Chrissie is there and has gone in and put the lights on. I hope the heating has come on. It would have been depressing to arrive to a cold, dark, empty house.

I get out of the car as Chrissie opens the front door and on seeing her, I cry again.

'Oh love, come here.' She hugs me, letting me cry for a few seconds before saying, in typical Chrissie style, 'Can we cry inside? I'm freezing my tits off out here.'

Settled with a strong drink (not tea this time) and a great friend, I turn my phone on. There are 3 text messages from Phil (still tingling) and a voicemail from Andy.

I decide to get the worst over and listen to Andy's message. I put it on loudspeaker, so Chrissie can hear too.

'Hi Amanda love. I know I'm the last person you want to speak to, but I just wanted to check you were erm … OK. I'll try you again later. Great news about Ellie and Jackie though. Also, erm … there's something I want to talk to you about and erm … I'll try you again later. I've already said that, erm ... OK, bye.'

'Hi Amanda love? Love? I'll give him fuckin' hi love!' Chrissie is fuming. She is a great person to have on your side and I know she would fight to the end for me, but I would hate to be on the other side.

'What do I do?' I'm still shaking but the brandy is helping. 'I'm not sure I want to speak to him and what the hell does he want to tell me? If he couldn't tell me in person that he's moving to sodding Australia, what the hell is he going to tell me now?' I feel sick and tell Chrissie.

She puts the kettle on (what can I say, tea soothes me) and finds an unopened, can you believe it, packet of biscuits.

'Sugar's good for shock so you have the tea and I'll have the brandy.' I can see she's rattled.

'What do I do?' I ask again. 'Do I ring him? Do I wait for him to ring me? Do I ignore him and tell him to speak through my Phil, I mean my solicitor?' Chrissie smiles at my faux par but doesn't say anything thankfully.

'You could ring him now, while I'm here if that helps or leave it for a few days. If he rings just ignore the call and give yourself a few days to get used to the idea of speaking to him and then we can call him together. And, if he's being a knob which is probably highly likely, I can tell him where to go.' I can see she's dying to do that bit.

'I'll leave it a few days like you say and then we'll ring him together.'

'Fair enough love. I'm here when you need me.' Chrissie gives my hand a squeeze.

'What was he on about Ellie and Jackie?' she asks, dipping her biscuit in her brandy. (What a waste of a good biscuit.)

I tell Chrissie all about the engagement and she's as happy as I am. We talk about the surprise/not surprise party for Audrey and Terry and that I've found a B&B for us all to stay in. I know she's looking forward to the party and a weekend away with Simon is always a bonus.

'There's something else I want to tell you. It's not a definite, but it's a definite maybe.' I pause as the words have vanished on my tongue.

'You're moving to Cornwall.' When I don't answer, she rolls her eyes. 'Do you think I'm daft or something?'

'No, but you're the only reason I would stay.'

'First of all, the only reason?' She gives me "the look".

'Ok, not the only reason but it's the only one I'm using right now.'

'Look, don't you think I can see how different you are when you're down there? Of course I'm going to miss you, I see you every day, but maybe I'll move down there too. I do have to win back the karaoke trophy.' She winks and reaching out, she puts her hand on my arm. 'I'm proud of you Mand and you should be proud of yourself too. You've had a hell of a time and are handling it better than anyone could imagine, and we deal with things like this all the time. We'll just forget about you sitting in Andy's smelly dressing gown surrounded by biscuit wrappers and cups of tea!' She laughs as I cringe at the memory.

'I've definitely come a long way from there, that's for sure.'

I pop a frozen pizza in the oven and I tell her about the cottage I've found and my new friend, Harriet.

'It sounds ideal. Maybe you could even set a practice up there?'

We agree to go back there when we go the party, so she can see the house and meet my mischievous new friend.

'I don't think I've said this but thank you.' I say to Chrissie as she prepares to leave.

'What for?'

I count the reasons off on my fingers.

'Showing me that I can go on. Helping me to see change as a positive thing. Prising Andy's dressing gown from me. Getting my hair and face sorted. Seeing that comfortable is a dirty word…. the list is endless, and I honestly can't thank you enough.' I give her a hug as she pats my back before pushing me away.

'Give over you daft cow.' She replies brusquely, but her rapid blinking gives away her feelings. 'I was just sick of walking around with an old lady.' Laughing I hug her again.

'Oh, I forgot to ask about Phil. Any more messages?' She smiles, but I tell Chrissie that I'll read them later.

'Spoilsport!'

We say goodnight as she heads off back to Simon, who's warming the bed up (too much information) and I unpack, run myself a bath and read Phil's messages while it's filling.

Hi, papers are with the courts and I'm just waiting for a date for the Nisi. P x

Hi again, I assume you're driving home now. Hope you have a safe journey. Speak to you soon. P x

P x! I know it's only an x but still. I send a quick reply saying I'm home safe and will speak to him tomorrow. (Go me taking control.) Is it ethical to date your solicitor? I'm sure he will know the answer to that better than me, besides we aren't dating. We are friendly, that's all. Friendly is good and ethical. AND I'm moving to Cornwall, well thinking of moving. Am I just thinking?

I know the answer to that but why does life have to be complicated? I would give anything for comfortable right now. Or would I? I recap what's happened this year.

- Andy leaves me – I fall apart
- Chrissie helps rebuild me – I sound like the bionic woman!
- Get gorgeous, sexy (OK I said it) solicitor – spark, definite spark (and tingles)
- New me has holiday – makes new friends and tries new things.
- Life continues back home – new me thinks of bigger picture/future
- Bumps into Phil outside of work – spark, tingle, wow
- Holiday again – Plan surprise party, make another friend, find a house (potentially)
- Andy rings – I fall apart
- Chrissie helps rebuild me – well, plies me with brandy, tea, biscuits and sage advice
- Gorgeous sexy solicitor text me – spark, definite spark (and tingles)

I am beginning to see a pattern emerging. I need to stop falling apart for one. It's not easy starting again when you thought that your comfortable life was mapped out already. But, do you know what? I can do it. This time I only had a mini breakdown. I don't know what Andy wants to talk to me about but whatever it is, I will handle it. I can't imagine what it would be that he feels he needs to tell me himself. Especially when he didn't tell me he was moving to the other side of the world.

Maybe she's pregnant. Oh God, maybe she IS pregnant. OK, breathe. In and out, in and out. No more breakdowns. At least the idea is there, so if it is that I won't be quite so shocked. It'll be harder for him to cope than me. I remember the broken sleep, school runs, swimming lessons, brownies and scouts … the list is endless. It makes me laugh because he was crap at it the first time around so decades later I don't imagine he'll be any better.

I go to bed with a smile on my face. This Mandy can kick arse and is not going to crumble each time there is a hurdle (well, not much anyway).

Chapter 24

It's the day of the party. Simon drove Chrissie and me down yesterday in his car, which meant I could see the view properly for the whole journey. Unfortunately, I wasn't allowed to bring Kenny or Dolly, but we had a laugh anyway. Well I did. Watching Chrissie gesticulating graphically at other drivers who were either too slow, too fast or god forbid, cut us up while Simon calmly ignored them, was hilarious and the journey seemed to fly by.

The Bed and Breakfast that we are staying in is called Rosemary Farm, and from I remember each room is decorated in a pastel theme with a patchwork throw on the bed and never-ending views of the frosty hills.

When we arrive, we are shown into the guest lounge where there's a roaring log fire and comfy sofas. Marjorie, the owner brought us a large pot of tea and some delicious biscuits that she made herself. She leaves us to warm ourselves and settle in. It was simply perfect. 10/10 for customer service.

As no one had met Simon yet, it was agreed that he would liaise with Gary and Mary regarding the venue and the cake and he would take the banner and enlarged photographs to the pub, where Gary would put them on display around the room. He was ordered to Facetime us when he got there so that we could see if anything needed tweaking. In all fairness it all looked gorgeous and Gary and Dean hadn't let us down.

Terry and I had spoken on the phone earlier to confirm that he was taking Audrey to the pub for a meal for her birthday and when they got there Gary would apologize and ask him to help with a lighting issue in the function room. The simple plan was that the lights would be off and knowing Audrey's inquisitive nature (nosy like me), she would go with Terry and once in the room Gary would switch the lights on and … SURPRISE!

In all honesty I think the one who will be most surprised is Terry and Audrey will be surprised that it's for Terry too. It should be a night to remember.

As everything was in hand and we had ages until the party, I took Chrissie to meet Harriet. We walk up the lane all wrapped up to the nines and breathing icy clouds as we go, and (as I knew she would) Chrissie fell in love with the place as soon as she saw it, just like I did. Coming back after just a few weeks, I forgot how gorgeous the place was.

I tell her my plans, obviously hypothetically if I go for it, and I mean IF.

'I'm thinking I would possibly knock down the garage and build an annex to the side for a private counselling practice. Obviously, the house would need renovating too but I'm in no rush to start a practice, so I can focus on the house first.'

'Hmm, it would be great, hypothetically of course.' She laughs, 'and, you wouldn't have a long commute.'

'It seems like it could be a good idea, but I still need to speak to the local hospices to see what they have in place and take it from there. Anyway, it's all …'

'Hypothetical, of course.' Chrissie laughs as she finishes my sentence.

'I don't know what you find so funny. I haven't fully made my mind up yet.'

'Not much.' She mumbles, but before I have time to argue Harriet opens the front door and welcomes us in. It's so lovely to see her again and she's thrilled to see us and to meet Chrissie.

'So, do you think she should buy it?' Harriet doesn't mince her words and goes straight to the point while putting the kettle on.

'Yes, I do, and I think it would be a great place to start over.' They chat as though I'm not even in the room. But it's not something you could take offence to as they are both smiling at me, waiting for me to commit to something I haven't even admitted to myself to doing.

'Honestly, you two!' I mock scold, bursting their conjoined bubble. 'Let's just see shall we. Anyway, first thing is tonight's party.'

'Party? Ooh, who's having a party?' I tell Harriet all about the double surprise for Audrey and Terry.

'Do you mean Audrey and Terry Booth?' she asks.

'Yes, why? Do you know them?' This is a small town indeed. It turns out that our dear mischievous Harriet used to teach them at their Junior School. She knew they'd married and had even bumped into them several times over the years, but she hadn't seen much of them recently.

'Oh, I have a wonderful idea,' I say, clapping my hands and squealing. (What? I can't be cool all the time). 'You should come to the party. I know they would both be thrilled to see you and on top of it, you get to have a great night out!'

'Oh, I don't know.' She's immediately flustered. This is the first time I've seen her lose her cheeky charm. 'I don't want to impose, and my hair would need doing. Goodness me, I haven't been to a party since the millennium, so I don't even know if my party dress will still fit me. No, I'll stay here, and you can come and tell me all about it tomorrow.'

'Bollocks' Chrissie's subtle approach is back. 'We can sort your hair out. We can wash it over the sink. You just get your dress out and we'll see if it fits so stop worrying. Ask Mandy, I'm great at makeovers.'

'But …'

'No buts!' Chrissie counters.

We have our tea and biscuits and I tell Harriet all about Ellie getting married and we all laugh as Harriet recounts some stories from her teaching days. As time is ticking on and we still need to get ourselves ready we get set on Harriet's makeover.

Within the hour Harriet is primped and preened to perfection and Chrissie and I feel like fairy godmothers. Her beautiful pale pink dress fits a treat, and now that she's ready I can see that Harriet is as excited as we are to be going to the party, and as a bonus get to see some of the children that she taught.

Back at the B&B we position Harriet in front of the fire to keep warm. Cup of tea in hand she shoo's us away so we can get ourselves ready.

After a quick shower, I blow dry my hair and carefully apply my make-up (Stella would be so proud). I feel great. I had my hair re-done last week and the colours shine beautifully in my wavy bob.

I bought myself a new dress for the party and was bowled over to find that a size 16 was too big! The 14 is a little snug (my body seems to favour clothing only sized with odd numbers as a 15 would be perfect), but I squeeze into it and feel rather sexy. It sits slightly off the shoulders with small sleeves, has a fitted waistline and is a fit and flare skirt stopping just at the knee. I slip on gold strappy heels and a delicate gold necklace and earrings, and I feel great. It's a shame really that no one (Phil) is going to appreciate it, but never mind, I'll definitely wear it again.

You're probably wondering what's happening with Phil. Well, to be honest nothing really. I plucked up the courage and rang him and said that I know there is something between us, but I would hate him to get into trouble as he's my solicitor. If we get the Decree Absolute and Christmas out of the way, and we still feel the same in the new year, then maybe we could go for a drink. I couldn't believe I was so grown up about it. Granted I'm 47 and should be grown up by now, but please don't judge.

Phil reluctantly said he agreed and he would definitely and categorically feel the same way, and he looked forward to the new year and new beginnings.

So, back to tonight. Simon and Chrissie make a gorgeous couple. Simon with his dark jeans and pale blue shirt and Chrissie in her black cocktail dress and heels are stunning, I feel great and Harriet looks amazing. The excitement is building as we 'Uber' our way to the party.

The room looks beautiful. It's all decorated with a Christmas theme, with fairy lights strung across the ceiling and around the walls and there's tinsel everywhere. Gary has even bought a real Christmas tree, which is twinkling in the corner. Dean has the food under control and has even done an extra dish of Chilli con carne and rice, to warm us all on this frosty night. But, the masterpiece is the three-tiered cake that our wonderful Mary has done. I never doubted for one minute that she wouldn't be up to the task, but she has truly excelled herself as the cake is simply stunning. Each layer alternates between gold and burgundy and the picture frames are all made of icing scrolled and piped to perfection. She has even managed to find Kenny and Dolly miniatures and placed a happy birthday banner in their hands, so it looks like they are holding it above their heads. She is one creative lady and I can't wait to tell her so.

There are about forty people in the room, some I recognise, but most I don't. There is a gentle hum of conversation as people are greeting each other, but I don't want to talk too loud in case Audrey can hear when she walks in.

Dean pops his head in from the kitchen to tell us they've arrived. We switch off the Christmas tree lights, fairy lights and the ceiling lights and then there's silence. My heart is beating so loudly that I think it'll give us all away. I can just hear Gary talking to Terry (who sounds like he's auditioning for a pantomime).

'I'm sorry to drag you away before you even get to your table but I've a problem with the lights in the back room.'

'Can't it wait Gary? We're on a night out.' We can all hear Audrey giving Gary what for.

'IT'S OK MATE,' says Terry (I really need to talk to him about his acting skills). 'A PROBLEM WITH THE LIGHTS EH?' I just know that he'll be scratching his head to emphasise his statement.

'I hope we get a free bottle of wine out of this Gary, it is my birthday meal after all that you're interrupting!' Audrey, typically feisty and nosy has tagged along as predicted. 'It's pitch black Gary; don't you have a torch? I don't want my Ter ...'

Gary reaches over to flick the lights on as we all shout 'SURPRISE!'

I don't know who is more shocked. Audrey, me (with the fact that Audrey hadn't guessed even with Terry's terrible acting) or Terry, who is totally speechless and hasn't closed his mouth yet and is looking at the birthday banner which says in big bold letters;

HAPPY 60th BIRTHDAY AUDREY AND TERRY! WE LOVE YOU XX

I go over to them and Audrey shrieks my name and gives me a huge hug for being here and how did I know? Then she looks at Terry who is still staring at the banner.

'How? Why?' He looks at me with unshed tears in his eyes and Audrey is looking at us both in amazement.

'Terry?' Audrey looks at her husband with so much love it makes my eyes fill up. 'Did you do this?'

'I don't know.' He looks at me again and then at the banner.

'I'll tell you quickly but then you both need to go and see your guests. Audrey, Terry wanted to do a surprise party for you and asked me to help.'

'I only had a packet of balloons.' He mumbles.

'I went to see Mary, who told me it was Terry's birthday a few weeks after yours and you would both be celebrating your 60th so we came up with the idea to have a surprise/surprise party, so she invited some extra people …'

'I only had a packet of balloons.'

'…and we came up with the rest one morning.' At this I am swamped in a group hug with Audrey and Terry, who's tears are now running down his face. Audrey is crying and then I'm crying and my carefully made up face is getting ruined. I pull away and wipe Terry's face with my hands. 'Now I want you both to go and enjoy your party. See your guests and have a drink.'

Terry gets hold of my hands and I can see the emotion in them.

'Thank you love,' he gives them a squeeze. 'I can't believe you did all this for Audrey and me.'

'It was an absolute pleasure, and remember it wasn't just me.' I give him a quick hug before I blub all over him and push him towards his wife, who's already chatting to her guests.

The DJ starts playing some 60's music and the buzz of chatter and laughter is intoxicating. I'm so happy to have been part of it and to give something back to this loving couple.

I pat my tears away with a tissue and look around the room. Harriet is having a little party of her own, with a string of guests wanting to pay their respects to their well-loved teacher. There's not a sad face or an empty glass.

Talking about empty glasses, Chrissie comes over with a couple of G&T's and gives me a hug. 'You did good kid, even I shed a tear and I'm a tough nut. Seriously, I think that this is your place to be.' I take a drink of my amber nectar and look around, when suddenly she holds me firmly by the shoulders and says, 'Don't think about it, just let it happen.'

'Let what hap ...' I haven't a clue what she means, but before I can finish she turns me around towards the door and standing there is Phil. I can't speak. She's reached over and taken my glass away. I don't understand what's going on and I probably resemble a goldfish, but then he's smiling and I'm smiling and the next thing I know he's up close and looking at me as though this is the first time he's seen me.

'Hi.' He says.

'Hi.' I say.

'You are breath taking.' He says.

I giggle and blush.

'I hope you don't mind me being here.' (As if.) I'm smiling at him and haven't taken my eyes away from his beautiful blue eyes and there is tingling, definite tingling. 'I know I said I would wait until the new year, but I just couldn't and then Chrissie rang to ask me when I was going to man up and stop pussyfooting around and she invited me to this party, so I drove down and am officially no longer pussyfooting around.'

We're still gazing at each other and I'm still in shock. The room goes quiet, the music and chatter fading, he's leaning forward ever so slowly and like a magnet so am I. This is the moment. He's going to kiss me, he's going to kiss me! I lean in to meet him in the middle.

'PHIL!' shouts Terry, who's suddenly bounding over and slapping Phil on the back.

'Huh?' I reply, bad timing or what. 'Terry? Phil? You know each other?'

'Course we do!' Grins Terry. 'He's got the holiday cottage a bit further down the beach. Have you got that lovely dog of yours with you?'

'Huh?'

'Oh, he's called Scruff,' Terry proceeds to tell me. 'and he's a …'

'A large sandy coloured … erm … what breed is he?'

Now it's Phil's turn to look confused, so I tell him about my earlier encounter with Scruff. 'I was down here earlier this year and he came bounding over and sat in front of me. By the time I'd gathered my stuff to see who his owner was, he had run back to you, but as you can gather, I didn't see you.'

'I guess fate was playing a hand.' Phil is smiling his dazzling smile at me and his eyes are bright with happiness. Suddenly, we both seem aware that we have an audience. Terry is standing there with a huge grin on his face.

'Oh yes, sorry Terry, I've left him at the cottage as I wasn't sure Gary would be thrilled with me bringing him in here and devouring the buffet. Anyway, Happy birthday mate.' He shakes Terry's hand and asks where Audrey is. Just before he goes off to see everyone who I didn't know he knew, he leans over and softly whispers in my ear, 'We'll continue this later.' He gently kisses my cheek and goes off in search of Audrey.

OH. MY. GOD. I swoon, actually swoon. I have never swun, swooned … whatever the hell it is, I am definite I have never done it. I turn to look for Chrissie but she's already on her way over, grinning and clapping. Even Simon is grinning. Before I can ask anything, Chrissie has enveloped me in a hug and smiling says, 'New beginnings start whenever and wherever you make them start. All I did was give fate a helping hand. You didn't mind, did you?'

'I love you my bezzie mate.' Was all I needed to say.

'I fuckin' love you too, yer daft cow.'

Epilogue

You are probably wondering about a lot of things right now. Did I move to Cornwall? What did Andy want? Did Phil and I 'get it on'? Am I still addicted to McVities?

First, I couldn't decide when to ring Andy, so I thought I would wait until after the party (I admit I was chickening out a little), but he took the decision out of my hands.

I had booked to get my hair re-coloured and cut for the party and I had seen a dress I liked in Harvey Nichols, so I was going shopping straight after. As usual they did a fantastic job and after buying the perfect party dress I was feeling particularly good. My hair was bouncy and gorgeous, and I'd had my nails done too. I pulled into my drive singing, as usual along to Kenny. My voice died instantly in my throat when I saw Andy with his hands in his pockets on our doorstep.

Had I not had my hair done I might not have felt so confident, but who knows. I got out of the car and I was thankful I had my new skinny jeans on, knee high boots (with a killer heel) and my wool coat. I looked and felt good and far different from the wife he'd left behind.

'Hello Andy.' I tried to hide my shock as I unlocked our front door, but my hands were shaking so much I think they gave away my nerves. I tried to put the fact that it was once 'our' front door to the back of my mind. This was no longer the case, Andy had put pay to that.

'You look … different.' He said. You look different? Wow, that's a hell of a compliment. I swallowed my reply and asked him what he wanted.

'I needed to talk to you and you wouldn't answer the phone. I've been ringing you for weeks Amanda. Anyway, I thought I'd come here and wait. I'm bloody freezing, but I didn't want to just let myself in.' What was he expecting? Praise? Sympathy? I had no idea and I didn't ask. Plus, I'd had the locks changed. Why didn't he just wait in the car. Idiot

'Well, it's summer in Australia so when you get there you'll be complaining you're too hot, I'd make the most of being chilly.' I couldn't resist. Bloody arsehole. 'Can you just tell me what you want Andy? I have plans and need to get ready.'

'Right erm … OK, the thing is …' I could see how uncomfortable he was and although it was great to see him lost for words, realisation dawns on me that I can't be bothered to listen to him.

'If you're here to tell me that Zooey is pregnant then say it and leave.' I didn't break eye contact and I saw confusion and then confirmation written on his face.

'How did you know?'

'I didn't but thanks for confirming it. I should be grateful you told me at all and hadn't got one of the kids to do it. Now if you don't mind I would be happier if you would just leave.' I stood there waiting for him to turn and go. 'Oh, there's a point, do the kids know?'

The look on his face told me the answer and his reply of 'I hoped you would do it' made me laugh out loud.

'Do you know what? You really are a pathetic man. First you get Molly to tell me and the others that you're moving to Australia, and now you want me to tell our children that they are going to have a half brother or sister?' I've edged towards him without me realising it. I am literally eye to eye with him (it's the killer heels).

'Have you seen them recently? Or are you just going to move to Australia, with no thought for them or your grandchildren?'

'Look I came because I thought I was doing the right thing. If you're going to be unreasonable, I'm just going to leave.'

Finding himself backed into a corner he resorted to his usual strategy and came out fighting.

'That's the best thing you've said since you opened your mouth.' I said, opening the front door. When he was outside he turned around and tried to make things better.

'Look, I'm sorry that came out all wrong.'

'Andy.' I said.

'Yes?' He said.

'Fuck off.' And with that I closed the door on him and my old life.

I won't lie, I crumbled to the floor at that point as the adrenaline had worn off. I know I thought Zooey was pregnant but hearing him confirm it wasn't so great and the thought of telling the kids didn't fill me with joy either, but do you know what? I would do it. I didn't like it, but I am a stronger person that I was earlier in the year and my children are far stronger and more insightful than I ever gave them credit for.

I stood up. Dusted my bum off and went to put the kettle on. What can I say? I can't change everything.

I put the house on the market the week after I came back from Cornwall (yes, I know you knew I would do it) and even though the estate agent said it wasn't the best time to sell a house, it sold within the first week. As Andy was leaving for Australia in the new year, he was in a rush to sell his business. I still can't believe that he would give it up so easily after all the hard work that went into making it the company it had become. But it was quickly snatched up by a competitor, and even though it sold quite a bit under the asking price, financially I am now a very comfortable lady. It's a nice feeling to be sat on a large nest egg and be able to do what I want, when I want.

As planned my children all came to stay for Christmas, and it was wonderful. The little ones played more with the boxes and wrapping paper than their gifts, but that's kids for you. We all had a wonderful time and ate far too much. Chrissie and Simon came around Christmas night and we played games and drank into the small hours. It was a perfect time and I would remember it forever.

The children and I had a long talk about their dad, their upcoming half-brother/sister and they were fine. Don't misunderstand me they were all upset, and it hit Ellie the hardest as I knew it would. Andy had always been on a pedestal for Ellie and to watch him fall off it all over again hurt her deeply. Luckily, she has Jackie and the rest of us, plus she knows a great counsellor and is talking to Chrissie regularly, she doesn't want to upset me and it's far easier to talk someone who's more detached. Not forgetting that she has a wedding to plan, which will take her mind of other issues.

I also took the opportunity to ask my wonderful children whether they would mind if I moved to Port Isaac and they were all genuinely happy for me, even saying I might meet someone who would treat me right. Little did they know how close that was to happening.

Before they left, they helped me pack up some of their old keepsakes that I had saved over the years. Now they could take them to their own homes and show them to their children when and if the others had them. The hardest part was when they all had to say goodbye to the home that they had grown up in. A few more tears were shed, but they are all looking forward to visiting me on the west coast.

I handed my notice in at work in the new year, which was a tearful affair, but if counsellors have one thing on tap, it's tissues. It was hard leaving everyone behind, especially Chrissie, but I needed a fresh start and she knew that more than anyone; besides, she had promised to be a regular at the local Karaoke.

I'm sure you guessed right but yes, I bought Harriet's beautiful house and she got her warden-controlled bungalow in the village that she had coveted for years. I am currently in the middle of re-wires, damp proofing, a new roof and I am having an annex built for my counselling practice. My life is better than I could ever have imagined.

You're probably wondering what happened with Phil. Well, you'll have to wait for an update on that as I'm not quite ready to share. One thing I can tell you is … he still makes me tingle.

~~The End~~
The Beginning

Printed in Great Britain
by Amazon